A Sweet Pea
IN BALTIMORE

LORI LUPUL

For the Loved Ones,
their family and friends,
and all the angels who work in harm reduction.

Chapter One

JADA CHECKED THE TIME ON her iPhone. It was 1:15 p.m. Thankfully, the bus she rode in was not too crowded. It was Tuesday, July 8, 2014, and she was on her way to the University of Baltimore to try out for the girls' cheerleading squad. Registration for tryouts began at two o'clock sharp, but Jada was not overly concerned about being late. Her chaperone, Cutty, whose real name was Chad Jones, had attended the university a couple of years prior. Cutty managed a local boxing club Jada's cousin, Brodie, belonged to. In fact, Brodie was the one who had asked Cutty to accompany Jada to her tryout, since Brodie was scheduled to start his new job at Coleman's Plumbing and Electrical the same day.

"How are you holding up, Jada?" Cutty glanced at her.

"Well, aside from a few butterflies in my tummy, I'm okay," she replied. "Thanks for tagging along. I really appreciate it."

"It's all good. Besides, the gym is gonna be quiet all week, what with school being out and the long weekend just over." Cutty ran his fingers through his short beard. "I'm expecting Brodie there after work. I sure hope it goes well for him."

"Me too!" Jada flashed Cutty one of her brilliant smiles.

She hadn't known him very long. She'd been working out at the boxing gym for about a month, mainly using the cardio equipment and weights. Brodie had asked Cutty's permission for Jada. She had taken dance lessons most of her life and had wanted some extra conditioning to prepare for cheerleading tryouts. Cutty had been game. The main purpose of the gym was to give local Baltimore youths a positive and safe outlet for fitness. Besides, Jada lived with Brodie and his mom, Ruby, so she was in the vicinity.

Recently graduated from high school, Jada was an honor student who had received a full scholarship to attend the University of Baltimore. She was enrolled in the undergraduate program in commerce, majoring in accounting. Jada's goal was to eventually study law and perhaps one day practice real estate law. She had been advised to take some accounting courses and be prepared to write well. Essays and research papers would be endless in postsecondary education.

Dancing was Jada's true passion, and she was no stranger to competition. It was Miss Henry, her guidance counselor at Doris M. Johnson High School, who suggested that Jada get involved in the cheerleading squad. Jada had thought, *Why not try out?* It would be a good distraction from her core courses, not to mention a way to meet people and expand her social circle.

Jada was all about having a balanced life. She had worked hard throughout her junior and senior years at school. Her dedication to her studies had been rewarded with the generous scholarship, and she felt blessed. Her drive to succeed had been fueled, in part, by a deep desire to avoid all the distractions that befell young girls. Jada had also been influenced by her high school's motto, "Success is the only option." But she had turned eighteen years old and was eager to embrace adulthood and all the magical elements it entailed.

The bus stopped in front of the recreation center. After the first few seats cleared, Cutty stood and allowed Jada to exit before him.

"After you," he pronounced. "It's showtime, shawty!"

"Okay, let's do this." Jada still felt butterflies in her tummy but didn't want to appear daunted. *Better put my best foot forward.*

The pleasant scent of Cutty's cologne did not go unnoticed as she passed him. Some of the boys in high school wore too much of the trendiest fragrances, which irritated Jada. But it wasn't in her nature to offend anyone, so she kept that information to herself.

As Jada stepped off the bus, she was impressed by the massive oak trees standing between her and the facility's entrance. These deciduous trees were among the most striking features of the University of Baltimore environs, a landmark for almost a century.

"Can you hear the birds singing, Cutty? They're the Baltimore orioles… the state bird, actually."

Cutty grinned. "Sure can! They're singing you a welcoming song today."

"Well, I don't know about that," Jada replied. "Did you know they live in Florida and Central America during our winter?"

"Smart birds," Cutty replied.

A few young people hung around the recreation center's grounds. As the pair approached the entrance, the door swung open as a middle-aged woman exited. Cutty was quick to grab the door and hold it for Jada.

Once inside, Jada looked for the women's locker room. She had worn a lacy light-blue sundress and planned on changing into her activewear for the tryouts.

"All right, this is where we part ways. I'll meet you back here at four?"

"Sure thing. But if I'm done early, how will I find you?"

Cutty extracted his iPhone from his pocket and suggested they share numbers. "Just text me if I'm not here."

Once they exchanged contact information, Cutty placed his right hand on Jada's upper left shoulder and gave it a light squeeze. "Good luck."

A deep tingling coursed through Jada's body. Looking up into Cutty's warm brown eyes, she replied, "Thanks, I'll need it." With that, Jada quickly turned, her backpack lightly brushing Cutty's chest, and headed toward the locker room.

With two hours to himself, Cutty bought a water bottle from the nearby vending machine and headed outside. It was eighty-two degrees with not a cloud in the sky. He strolled the expansive grounds toward the education building, where he had earned his bachelor's in physical education just two years before. He'd chosen well and could see how taking the pause year before starting college had given him time to figure out what he wanted to do. Cutty had tried his hand at a couple of jobs, including construction and as a security guard. Managing the gym was a nice balance between the physicality of construction work and the quiet, reflective time of monitoring a building after hours.

Cutty remembered his classmates as he studied their graduation photo on the main level near the elevators. A few of them had managed to obtain teaching jobs in public schools throughout Baltimore. This was a huge feat since budget cuts in the education system had been ongoing for some time. According to Mayor Rossi's most recent announcement, education funding was not the priority, even though it had been a part of his platform.

Instead, the Baltimore City Police department would receive more government money since crime was steadily rising. Cutty believed education was a huge factor in steering the youth from a life of crime, which, in Baltimore, stemmed from the long-standing illicit drug trade. The government should give both the police department and education equal funds.

Cutty's early childhood experience had left him a little jaded when it came to drugs. His birth mother had died of a heroin overdose when he was two, which had sent him into foster care. He'd never known his father. At twelve, he'd been recruited by the Bradly gang, where he'd learned to sling dope. His one-month stint had ended abruptly after police raided the street corner he worked. Shaken, Cutty had spent one night in a juvenile detention center. If not for the intervention of a tenacious social worker, Cutty most likely would have ended up back on the streets, living a life of crime.

After ambling around the education building, Cutty made his way back to the recreation center. Once inside the foyer, he found a comfortable seat and spent some time on his iPhone. He browsed Twitter and caught up on the current sports tweets.

The doors to the foyer entrance opened, and two male students walked in. They approached Cutty, and the taller one spoke. "Yo, have tryouts ended?"

"Not quite, but I suspect they'll be over shortly."

"Thanks," the tall one replied.

The two men walked away.

Cutty couldn't help but notice how attractive and polite the young men were. Judging by the shorts and tank tops they wore, Cutty was certain they were basketball players. *Jada will have the pick of the litter.*

Only a few people waited inside the foyer. The gymnasium suddenly went quiet as the dance music he'd heard when he first entered the building stopped. The judges were probably making their final decisions. Cutty wondered how Jada fared.

A few minutes had passed, and Cutty began to follow some local news. More Mayor Rossi tweets defending the budget plans.

Cutty felt a subtle shift in the air. He looked up and saw Jada standing in front of the gymnasium door, about twenty feet in front of him. Their eyes locked. She slowly held up a white envelope in front of her. Her smile erupted. *That's a good sign.*

Jada ran toward Cutty, and he stood just in time to catch her as she jumped into his arms. Cutty gently set Jada on her feet and planted a soft, reflexive kiss on her forehead.

"You made the squad?" Cutty asked.

"Yeah… I can hardly believe it. It was so exciting!" Jada exclaimed.

Cutty slowly let his hands drop from Jada's waist, and she took a small step back.

"Congratulations! I'm sure you blew all the judges away." Cutty couldn't help feeling proud of Jada as he grinned from ear to ear. "You must be hungry. Would you like to get a snack before we head to the bus station?"

"I would love that. But first, I need to change. I'll just pop into the locker room. Give me ten minutes?"

"Sure thing. I'll wait here." Cutty sat in his seat.

As Jada headed toward the locker room, she quickly group-texted her aunt Ruby, Brodie, and her friend Chloe the good news. Once inside, she changed back into her sundress and freshened up. The large bun atop her head had held up fairly well during the competition. But she was used to putting up her long tresses and knew how to secure a hairdo or two. Before she left the locker room, Jada took a deep breath. She silently thanked God for her success. She couldn't help but think that her freshman year was going to be amazing.

Cutty stood up as Jada walked toward him. "I thought we'd head over to the food court. There'll be a few choices there."

"Lead the way, please! I'm starting to feel a little shaky. Need to boost my blood sugar," Jada replied gratefully.

As they walked toward the food court, Jada filled Cutty in on some of the dance drills she'd had to perform for the judges. Some were a little tricky, but she'd given it her best, all the while keeping a smile on her face.

Once inside the food court, Jada noticed Jamba Juice. "I'd love a smoothie!"

"Sounds good, shawty, but it's my treat."

Jada ordered the peanut-butter-and-banana protein smoothie, thinking it would satisfy her hunger until suppertime.

Cutty ordered the banana-berry smoothie with a purple hue.

"Do you like berries?" Jada asked.

"I sure do love me some blueberries. They're full of antioxidants and nutrients."

Just before heading out the door, Jada placed her left hand gently on top of Cutty's right forearm. "Thank you for the smoothie, Cutty. I'm so glad you came to the tryouts with me. You were my lucky charm!"

"You're welcome. But I had nothing to do with your success. That's all on you. I suspect you must be one heck of a dancer too." Cutty and Jada sauntered toward the bus stop, smoothies in hand.

Chapter Two

T HE NEXT MORNING, JADA WOKE to the soft ping of her iPhone.

Hey, girl, when can you hang? It was a text from Chloe, her best friend since second grade.

Chloe's family owned a small local grocery store, where she and her twin brother, Michael, worked part-time. Chloe had registered for the nursing program at the University of Maryland beginning in the fall. Michael hoped to become an electrician, like his friend Brodie, but he needed to find an apprenticeship position first.

How about after lunch? We could hit up Macy's one-day sale, baby! Jada got out of bed and headed downstairs to the kitchen, where she was greeted by a garlicky aroma.

"Good morning, Aunty. What are you cooking today?"

"Good morning, Jada. I'm making a double batch of lasagna. One for us and one for Cutty. Just a little something to thank him for escorting you to the cheerleading tryouts yesterday."

"Aw, Aunty… that's so sweet of you." Jada gave her aunt Ruby a side hug. "I'm heading to the gym after breakfast, so I can take it to him if you like."

"Sounds good. There's a little bit of coffee left if you'd like to have some with your peanut butter toast," Ruby suggested.

"Oh, perfect. I'm starving." Jada headed to the toaster. "Do you have any plans for today?"

"Mm-hmm. Once I finish cooking, I plan on heading downstairs to work on my quilt. It'll be nice to escape this heat for a while." Ruby was an avid seamstress and had set up a lovely room in the basement for her quilting projects.

"Nice. I'll wash the dishes once I'm finished eating."

"Thanks, sweetie. I can always count on you."

At three years old, after losing her mother, Dawn, to stomach cancer, Jada had moved in with her aunt Ruby and uncle Roy. It had taken Ruby and Roy so long to conceive their son, Brodie, that they had welcomed the idea of adopting Jada. Roy had worked as a longshoreman for the Port of Baltimore. Sadly, he had passed away in a work accident when Jada and Brodie were ten years old.

Jada put on some gray cropped leggings and a purple tank top and headed to the gym. She spotted Cutty standing beside the boxing ring. He was watching intently as two boys sparred. Cutty wore black shorts and an olive-green tank top.

"Hey, Cutty."

Cutty turned from the ring. "Oh, hey, Jada. Are you working out this morning?"

"Yeah. I thought I'd workout Monday, Wednesday, and Friday mornings… well, at least, I'll aim for that, if it's okay with you."

"Fine by me. And that sounds like a good schedule. A girl's got to pace herself." Cutty winked.

Jada grinned. "Not too many boys in here today?"

"Nah, the boys just want to hang outside in all the nice weather."

"Yeah, I can't blame them. Now that my dance lessons have ended, I need to step up my game in order to keep in shape for the cheer squad."

"I feel you. And I can help you set up a program, you know… weights and all, if you are interested in targeting specific muscle groups."

"Would you? That would be awesome!" Jada was pleased. "I'll just start by doing twenty minutes on the elliptical. Then maybe we can go over my biceps and triceps routine today… see if it needs tweaking?"

"I'd be happy to," Cutty acknowledged.

One of the boys in the ring cried out, and Cutty turned to see him fall to the floor. Cutty jumped up and climbed over the ropes in a heartbeat and helped the boy get up. Once Cutty assessed the situation, he murmured a few words of advice. The boys sipped from their water bottles and got right back to sparring. Cutty climbed out of the ring and jumped down beside Jada.

"Close call. I shouldn't distract you. My aunt Ruby made you a lasagna." Jada placed the casserole dish in Cutty's hands.

"No way! Why'd she do that?" Cutty looked pleasantly surprised.

"It's her way of thanking you for taking me to the university."

"Well, this is so kind of your aunt! You'll have to thank her for me. I'll just go put it in my fridge." Cutty walked toward his suite at the back of the gym. Then he stopped and looked at Jada. "You know, I enjoyed our outing yesterday. It's been a while since I've been to my alma mater. Brought back a few memories."

"Aw... I'm glad." Jada made her way to the cardio section and began with some warm-up exercises. A short while later, a couple of teenage boys arrived at the gym. They spoke with Cutty briefly then began their workout. One boy used the treadmill and the other used the stationary bicycle. After the boys completed ten minutes of cardio, Cutty helped them wrap their hands prior to using the punching bags. Cutty was adamant that the boys in his gym learn the proper techniques for all exercises and equipment. Wrapping was crucial, as it protected the hands and supported the wrists.

After Cutty watched the boys throw a few punches, he walked over to Jada. "Slow down as you lower the dumbbells," he suggested.

Jada did a few more reps of the biceps curls to finish her set.

"Do you know hammer curls?" he asked.

"Like this?" Jada turned the ten-pound weights perpendicular to her hips and slowly raised them just past ninety degrees.

"Just bend your knees a little. And remember to exhale on the way up…" *Whooo*, Cutty demonstrated with his breath. "That's it," he commented. "Now, give me fourteen more reps."

Jada did as she was told.

"Do you know concentration curls?" he continued.

Jada shook her head.

"Ah… they're good. We need the bench, though." Cutty picked up an eight-pound dumbbell and sat on the bench with his legs spread. "Rest the back of your upper arm against your inner thigh and lift the dumbbell." He demonstrated the movement then offered the weight to Jada.

She sat beside him, took the weight in her right hand, and slowly curled it all the way up to her chest.

"Make sure you lock your elbow in place as you come back down—don't hyperextend it."

Jada lowered the weight with control and locked her elbow.

"Nice," Cutty praised. "This exercise is really gonna hit the peak of the bicep. Here."

His skin felt warm and comforting as he gently touched her forearm.

Cutty spent time going over some triceps exercises with the dumbbells, all the while being patient and encouraging with Jada. The sound of his voice was dreamy to her. *I wish he could spot me for all my workouts.*

Once she completed her repetitions, Cutty headed back to the ring. He couldn't leave the boys alone for too long. Jada did some cooldown stretches. Before she left, she made eye contact with Cutty, waved, and mouthed a thank-you to him. He nodded in response.

Later that evening, Jada and Ruby cleaned up the kitchen together after enjoying lasagna and salad for supper. They poured some iced tea into two glasses and headed toward the living room so Jada could show her aunt a tank top and pair of shorts she had purchased earlier that afternoon with Chloe.

Suddenly, the front door swung open, and in walked Brodie and Cutty.

"Hey, ladies," Brodie greeted his mom and cousin. He wore his usual black do-rag. "Smells good in here." He headed toward the kitchen to help himself to supper.

He had just finished spending time at the gym after work, Jada suspected, and was ready to eat. It appeared Cutty had joined Brodie on his walk home, which was roughly three blocks from the gym.

"Hi, Cutty." Jada was pleasantly surprised to see him.

"Hi." It was Cutty's first time inside Ruby's town house. "Lovely home you have here." Cutty took in his surroundings. "Thanks for the delicious lasagna, Mrs. Parker." Cutty tipped his head toward Ruby.

"You are most welcome, Cutty. And please, call me Ruby." Ruby was quite vocal about her respect for Cutty, especially since he was a good influence on her son and his peers. "You'll have to come over for a barbecue sometime this summer."

"I wouldn't miss that," Cutty responded emphatically. "Brodie and some of the boys were talking earlier about getting together this Friday night for a volleyball game and barbecue over at Baltimore Beach. Care to join us, Jada? I'd appreciate some extra eyes on the younger kids."

"I'd love to," Jada replied. "Can I invite my friend Chloe?"

"Do it!" Brodie exclaimed from the kitchen.

"Sure. It'll be good having more players for the game." Cutty put his hand on the doorknob. "Well, thanks again. 'Night."

Jada got off the couch and walked toward the door. She followed Cutty outside and stood on the landing while he walked down the four concrete steps to the sidewalk. "I'll see you at the gym on Friday."

"All right. Great job on cooldown and stretches after your workout." Cutty looked intently up at Jada.

"Thank you." She met his gaze. "I do a little yoga off YouTube."

"Nice. I can show you some exercises for quads, check your squats and lunges."

"I look forward to it. Be safe," she added.

"Always." Cutty turned to walk home.

Chapter Three

THE PLAN ON FRIDAY WAS for everyone to meet at the boxing gym at four thirty. Cutty borrowed a 1995 Suburban that belonged to St. Peter's Evangelical Lutheran Church. He had a good relationship with the reverend, Joe Whittaker, or Rev Joe, as everyone called him. The reverend was very supportive of Cutty's undertakings because the latter showed a genuine interest in improving the local youths' morale.

Brodie and Jada walked together from their home. As they approached the SUV, Cutty loaded a cooler into the hatch. Several boys hung around on the sidewalk. One boy, D'andre, played his iTunes music while a few others grooved to the beat. The boys were obviously excited for their outing.

"Hey! Y'all excited to get your game on?" Brodie addressed the crowd.

"We sure are, Brodie!" Tyrell, another boy in the group, exclaimed.

"Now, which of you boys are taking the bus to the beach?" Cutty could only take another eight passengers in the SUV besides himself, as it seated nine. D'andre and Tyrell volunteered to take the bus and took two of the passes Cutty held up.

"I'll ride with these two... just to keep an eye on them," Brodie volunteered, also taking a bus pass.

"All right. We'll meet at the beach in about thirty minutes or so. Whoever arrives first, try to reserve a volleyball court. Everyone, make sure you have your belongings and take your seats in the Suburban. Remember to be respectful of this vehicle, as it belongs to the church!" Cutty turned toward Jada and softened his voice. "Would you like to ride in the front, honored guest?"

Jada giggled. "You mean 'only girl'?" She slid into the middle seat.

Cutty followed suit, taking the driver's seat. "Buckle up, everyone," he ordered, carefully checking all the mirrors. He looked over his shoulder prior to pulling out of the parking spot.

Jada sat so close to Cutty that she could feel the warmth from his right leg. She was impressed with how well he maneuvered such a large beast through the streets.

Once parked at Baltimore Beach, Cutty designated some of the boys to take volleyballs over to the unoccupied court while others helped unload the hatch. He had purchased an ample supply of water bottles, juice boxes, wieners, buns, condiments, chips, and marshmallows for the excursion with funds from a grant that supported the boxing gym. The grant, which also provided Cutty's wages, fell under the umbrella of the US Department of Health and Human Services.

It didn't take long to unload the hatch. The boys were anxious to play, so Cutty divided the group into two teams. Jada and Brodie played opposite Cutty. D'andre and Tyrell had played volleyball in school and, having just completed grade eleven, were pretty adept at the game. They were very encouraging to the younger boys.

Chloe and Michael arrived after the first game ended. Finally, Jada had some female support, as Chloe was assigned to her team.

The second game was intense. When it was her turn, Chloe executed a good serve, which Michael received and set the ball for Cutty. Cutty passed it over the net, and Jada was ready. Only five feet, five inches tall and one hundred seven pounds, she jumped high and spiked the ball near D'andre, who dove. But he missed as the ball hit the ground.

Cutty's team won the match as the third game ended. Everyone was hungry, so they headed to the firepit. Cutty started a small fire while the boys organized the food and beverages. Cutty picked up a bunch of wire coat hangers.

"What are those for?" Jada asked.

"These are what we'll cook the wieners on. As you can see, this ain't no Martha Stewart kitchen here."

Cutty gestured to the firepit. "Besides, the kids have to learn how to improvise."

"Can I try one?"

"Sure. You just undo the wire here then straighten the hanger like a stick." Cutty demonstrated the process to Jada.

Soon, the boys were cooking wieners. Since space and safety around the firepit were an issue, the older kids let the younger ones go first. Overall, the cookout turned out well. A couple of the wieners were cooked to a crisp, while one was dropped into the pit. For dessert, Cutty provided watermelon he had sliced ahead of time.

"Hot dogs cooked over an open fire are the best," Michael reported.

"Yeah, but 7-Eleven makes a pretty good dog too," Brodie responded.

Everyone laughed. One of the boys let out a rather large belch followed by some gaseous sounds emitted by another boy.

"All right, knock it off, boys! We are in the presence of ladies," Cutty ordered.

Jada was flattered, but she didn't mind the boys. They were just letting out some steam. She straightened her white tank top, pulling it down over her light denim shorts.

After tidying up, the kids thanked Cutty for their meal. Someone suggested they take a walk down around the Inner Harbor, where numerous boats were moored.

"Michael and I can supervise the boys, Cutty, if that's all right with you," Brodie offered.

"Okay. Boys, listen up. Stay together. Stay out of trouble, and listen to your elders," Cutty said seriously. "And be back here in thirty minutes."

The boys nodded in agreement, and the group headed away from the pit.

Chloe joined the walkers, while Jada stayed back to help Cutty load the supplies into the SUV. Once the chores were done, they sat down in two lawn chairs the reverend had supplied and took in the lovely sight around the water's edge.

"The evening turned out well, huh?" Jada probed.

"Not too bad. All I need to do now is get the boys home safe, then maybe I'll get a good night's rest."

They both laughed.

"And you play a pretty good game of volleyball, shawty!"

"Well, I sure felt more confident once my girl Chloe arrived."

"Yeah, she played pretty well too. I was amazed by the older boys' skills. It's good for the younger ones to experience that."

Jada nodded.

"Have you known Chloe a long time?"

"Oh yeah," Jada replied. "She and I go back to el-ementary school." Then she chuckled. "We used to think we were so smart in middle school... keeping tabs on what the other kids did, seeing them get into mischief and all. We stayed under the radar."

Cutty smiled.

"Then, once in high school, it was like we transformed. We motivated each other to do well in our studies. We were lucky because we always had Brodie and Michael looking out for us. Our mantra was ABC, 'always be classy.' At least, that's what Miss Henry taught us. She was our guidance counselor."

"Did Chloe take dance lessons with you?"

"Yes, during elementary and middle school. But she started working at her parents' store in high school. Same as Michael. Then Chloe started thinking about becoming a nurse, so she began volunteering at the hospital. I'm not sure what she's doing for exercise now."

"She's been coming to the gym in the evenings."

"She has?" Jada was astonished.

"Yeah. She works out while Brodie and Michael are training."

Interesting. Jada made a mental note to find out what was up with Chloe. "How about you, Cutty? Do you have many friends?"

"Yeah. I have a couple of friends from high school. Elias is a mechanic down at a garage on Fourth Street. He's got this really cool 2001 BMW he works on all the time. Keeps it all polished… it's sweet! He and his fiancée, Samantha, are getting married next summer. Elias asked me to be his best man."

"Aw." Jada smiled, noticing the happiness in Cutty's voice.

His demeanor changed. "Then there's our buddy Levi. He got into the drug scene when he was around twenty years old." Cutty appeared sombre. "He started out by using cocaine. And after a while, he switched to meth. But that just really messed with his head. We almost lost him."

"Oh no," Jada replied.

"Levi's doing better now. His rehab was a long process. Kind of two steps forward then one back. Withdrawal was pretty tough on him, and he experienced about a year of anhedonia... where he couldn't feel pleasure. It was frustrating for him. And he struggled with depression. Medication didn't help him, so he began to work out and watch his diet. He comes to the boxing gym, sometimes helps me with supervision, and he goes to Narcotics Anonymous meetings regularly. Elias and I, we help keep him straight."

"Have you ever tried drugs, Cutty?"

"Yeah. I smoked a bit of marijuana for a spell back in middle school. I thought I was cut out for the punk life back then. But that ended once I landed in juvenile detention." Cutty shook his head. "Social Services placed me in a foster home with an older couple, Marvin and Delores," he reflected. "Man, they were firm but loving, and they helped me turn my life around. I took their surname, Jones." He smiled. "Dad—that's what I call Marvin—encouraged me to get into football. I was so

23

fast during the forty-yard dash that I made first cut in tryouts." He chuckled. "That's how I got the nickname Cutty."

He looked at Jada and continued, "I tried a little cocaine back in my early twenties, when I partied with Levi. But all that did was keep me awake at night and give me a bad headache the next morning. I regret that now—made quite the dent in my bank account. But it could have been a lot worse." Cutty paused for a moment. "That's why I attend the occasional NA meeting with Levi."

"Wow," Jada murmured. "Thanks for sharing." If Jada had learned one thing in her eighteen and a half years, it was that no one had a perfect life. Even if someone appeared to be doing well, they could always be struggling in the background. It was best not to judge others too quickly.

Someone in a shiny blue four-door BMW sedan honked from the parking lot.

"Well, speak of the devil." Cutty stood. "That's Elias and Samantha. He said they might stop by tonight."

Jada recognized Elias from the gym as Cutty made the introductions.

Within a few minutes, the group returned from their walk. One of the boys' parents arrived to pick up his son and the son's friend. Michael and Chloe had their dad's car to drive home. Jada gave them each a quick hug goodbye while Cutty had the rest of the boys climb into the Suburban.

"Anyone need a ride home?" Elias offered.

D'andre and Tyrell were quick to accept, so Brodie joined Cutty's group in the SUV.

Upon returning to the gym, the boys began their routes home. Jada and Brodie helped unload the Suburban while Cutty unlocked the gym door. "Leave the lawn chairs in the SUV." He picked up the cooler and carried it toward his suite.

"Pardon me, are you the proprietor of this boxing gym?" someone with a loud voice inquired behind them.

The three of them turned to see a rather large gentleman dressed in a tan suit and tie make his way through the gym doors.

"Yes. Chad Jones—call me Cutty." He set down the cooler and walked toward the newcomer.

"I'm Detective Tommy Walker with Baltimore Homicide, Eastern District." He shook Cutty's extended hand. "Can you spare a few minutes?"

"Yes, sir," Cutty replied.

Detective Walker had their full attention.

"Earlier this evening, around five thirty, a Black teenage boy was murdered not quite four blocks south of here. It was a single gunshot wound to the back of the head. The Baltimore City Police are canvasing the surrounding area, searching for any witnesses or clues to this tragedy," Detective Walker stated.

"No!" Cutty exclaimed.

Jada gasped. Brodie was quick to console her, placing a hand on her back.

"I'm afraid so," the detective continued. "It's possible that he was a new recruit for a local gang... a victim of the ongoing turf war." The detective eyed all three. "Have you noticed anything suspicious around the gym tonight?"

"No, as a matter of fact, the gym was closed for the evening, since four thirty. My friends and I took some of the boys down to Baltimore Beach to play volleyball and have a wiener roast." Cutty gestured toward Brodie and Jada.

"You're just returning now?" The detective glanced at the cooler and bags.

"Yes, Detective," Cutty replied.

"All right. If you hear any information related to this incident, any detail at all, can you call this number?" The detective handed Cutty a card.

"Absolutely," Cutty responded.

With that, the detective bade them farewell and left.

"That's just not right." Brodie shook his head in disbelief.

"It's a real shame," Cutty agreed.

"Can we do anything for you?" Brodie asked.

"No. I'll return the Suburban to the church in the morning. I can't thank you both enough for helping me with the outing tonight," Cutty acknowledged solemnly.

"All right, thanks for everything. I'll see you soon." Brodie fist-bumped Cutty then turned to leave.

"Good night, Cutty. Take it easy." Jada gave a little wave.

"Thanks, you too, Jada." Cutty gave her a small grin.

Chapter Four

CUTTY AWOKE SATURDAY MORNING FROM a restless sleep. Although he was grateful the trip to Baltimore Beach the night before had been a success, a feeling of doom sat in the pit of his stomach. The news the detective had shared about the murdered boy really disturbed him. He slowly got up and made himself some breakfast.

Cutty drove the Suburban back to the church. He hoped to have a word with Rev Joe. As luck would have it, the reverend was sitting at his desk in the rectory.

"Good morning, Reverend. I brought the Suburban back in one piece." Cutty placed the keys on the desk.

"Good morning to you too. How was the wiener roast?" Reverend Joe was in his late fifties. Having devoted his life to the church and its parishioners, he had never married.

"It went well. I think the boys had a good time. They behaved themselves for the most part." Cutty gave a slight smile.

"Oh, glad to hear that. You know, this community is blessed to have you. I'm so proud of all you do for it, Cutty."

"Thanks." Cutty was touched. "It's really teamwork that makes things happen. Plus, I have the support of some of the older kids. I've told you before about them pitching in with supervision and filling in for me at the gym if I need to run an errand."

"You've mentioned Brodie Parker and Michael Smith," the reverend confirmed.

"Yeah, and Brodie's cousin, Jada, and Michael's sister, Chloe, helped out last night. Also, Tyrell and D'andre have really stepped up."

"Excellent. It's so good to see the Lord's handywork answering our prayers for the youth," the reverend replied knowingly.

Cutty nodded in agreement. "But I have to say my mood really turned once we got back to the gym last night. This detective showed up… asked if we knew anything about the young man shot and killed earlier in the evening—most likely drug related."

"It's a real tragedy, Cutty, such a waste of human life… a boy merely on the verge of adulthood and finding his path. The police stopped by the church last night. Once they identify the victim, I plan on visiting his family to get a sense of what kind of support and comfort I can offer them."

"Let me know if you hear any word about the victim and his family," Cutty responded respectfully. "I should be getting back to the gym now. It's almost opening time. Thanks again for lending me the Suburban last night and the extra goodies."

"My pleasure. And I will let you know if I hear anything. Take care, and be assured that the perpetrators will be held accountable." The reverend patted Cutty's arm.

"All right." Cutty turned and headed for the door. The five-block walk back to the gym would help clear his mind.

Jada spent her weekend cleaning her room and purging her closet. Chloe spent most of Saturday helping her. They had made a pact when school had ended to support one another with completing the daunting task. They planned to tackle Chloe's closet the following Saturday.

Chloe had heard the news about the young man's demise the previous evening, as the police had visited her parents' grocery store. She and Jada both agreed that everyone needed to be cautious about their surroundings while out and about. The turf war was getting too close for comfort.

"Cutty mentioned you've been working out at the gym in the evenings." Jada sought to lighten the mood.

"Yeah, I tagged along with Michael last week. He wanted to go when Brodie trained. I figured it was time to get myself in shape since I'll be buying nursing scrubs soon enough." Chloe chuckled. "Not to mention we'll be sitting at desks, studying most of the day."

"Good for you, Chloe. Let me know if you ever want to go to the gym with me in the mornings. Cutty has been so helpful. He's tweaked my routine some and helped me with my form."

"Okay, but it depends on my work schedule at the store," Chloe responded. "That Cutty is a fine man. And he's ripped!"

Jada grinned at the latter remark, a slightly impish flash of a smile.

A short while later, Brodie returned home with Michael in tow. They had worked out at the gym earlier then spent some time at the Smiths', where they'd searched online for electrical apprenticeships for Michael.

"Hey, girls, how's the deep cleaning going?" Brodie asked.

"It's coming along nicely, thanks for asking," Jada responded.

"When you girls are finished, you should help Brodie and me clean our rooms," Michael chimed in.

"No thanks," Chloe was quick to reply. "We'll leave that alone. Besides, you have more time on your hands than the rest of us." Chloe gave her twin brother a smirk.

"Michael and I ordered pizza. It should be here soon. You two are welcome to join us," Brodie offered.

"Sounds good! I'm ready for a break." Chloe beamed.

"Fair enough," Brodie said. "I told Mom to take the night off cooking. I'll let her know the pizza's almost here." He headed for the basement.

"Okay, I'll set the table and get some drinks," Jada offered.

Chloe helped her while Michael turned on the television in the living room to watch some sports.

After supper, Ruby watched television while the four younger adults hung out at the kitchen table. They enjoyed a couple rounds of rummy and chatted about their summer plans. Around ten o'clock, Michael and Chloe bade their farewells and departed for their walk home, a few blocks away.

By Monday morning, Jada was ready to be done with her room. She had managed to throw out a ton of old high school notes and unwanted knickknacks and set aside some clothes for donation. She donned some workout attire, form-fitting black nylon-spandex shorts with a gray tank top, and put her hair up in a high ponytail. Then she set out toward the gym.

Once inside the boxing gym, Jada noticed a Wanted poster issued by the Baltimore City Police on the bulletin board near the entrance. The victim of Friday night's shooting had been identified as sixteen-year-old Devon Lewis, whose picture appeared there. The police were offering a monetary reward for any information leading to the arrest of the perpetrator(s), and a phone number was listed on the sheet for citizens to call in, anonymously if they chose. The news saddened Jada. She immediately sought out Cutty.

"Good morning, Cutty." She found him sorting through boxing equipment. "How are you?"

"Good morning." Cutty stood from his task. "To tell you the truth, I've been better. You saw the poster?" He inclined his head toward the bulletin board.

"Yes. It's heartbreaking."

Cutty sighed. "Yeah. I really hope the police catch who did it soon."

"I couldn't agree more." Jada nodded. "Chloe and I were just saying how this turf war is too close to home. We need to be careful when we're out."

"That's a good point, Jada. I need to remind all the boys of that." Cutty appeared deep in thought.

"I'm going to start my workout now. Talk to you later?" Jada asked.

"For sure," Cutty replied.

When Jada returned to the gym on Wednesday morning, she noticed that Cutty still seemed a little preoccupied. Although he was polite to her, Jada could sense that his mood had shifted. By the time she finished working out, she had formulated a plan, and it was time to set it in motion. She walked over to the stationary bicycle, where Cutty was performing monthly maintenance.

"That looks tricky," Jada noted as Cutty lubricated the rear wheel.

"Oh, it's not too hard. The challenge is to not get grease on your clothing." Cutty held a can of WD-40 multipurpose lubricant. "You heading home now?"

"Yeah. Do you have any plans this Sunday?"

"This Sunday? I don't believe so." Cutty looked at Jada as he stood.

"Would you be interested in going to the zoo with me?" Jada asked demurely.

"The Maryland Zoo?" Cutty seemed surprised.

"Yeah, that one." Jada smiled. "It opens at ten. I thought we could go early, in case the day turns out to be a scorcher."

"Well, it's been a long time since I set foot in the zoo... I'm thinking a fifth-grade field trip."

"I go every summer. I just love the African Journey. I can ask Aunt Ruby to help me make a picnic lunch. That way, we just need to purchase our tickets and bus fare," Jada added.

Cutty pondered the information, creating an awkward pause.

"You don't have to decide this minute. Text me if you're interested." Jada turned to leave. "See you Friday."

"Sounds good." Cutty watched pensively as Jada walked toward the door and exited.

Once outside, Jada felt a soft, welcoming breeze. *Go big or go bust.*

After lunch, Jada received some good news. Cutty texted that he would be happy to go to the zoo with her. She smiled as she headed to the basement to discuss the menu with her aunt, certain that the outing was just what Cutty needed to cheer him up.

Cutty met Jada outside her town house on Sunday morning wearing denim Bermuda shorts with a navy T-shirt and canvas slip-on shoes. By coincidence, Jada had dressed in denim shorts with a navy paisley smocked tank top and silver flip-flops. Her aunt had plaited Jada's hair into two French braids that extended down her back. She carried a backpack on one shoulder.

"Good morning. I see you got the memo!" Jada exclaimed as she looked at Cutty's attire.

"Yeah, casual Sunday." Cutty chuckled. "You look nice."

"Thanks. So do you." Jada grinned.

They walked to the nearby bus stop. After transferring only once to another bus, they arrived at the zoo just after ten o'clock. After purchasing their tickets, Jada and Cutty walked the short distance to the zoo exhibits.

"I thought we'd start out with the African Journey, since it's my favorite," Jada suggested.

"Sure thing," Cutty agreed. "Lead the way."

Jada sensed that Cutty already seemed a little more at ease. She led them to the Penguin Coast Exhibit, which housed approximately fifty African black-footed penguins. They stood along the wire-and-wood railing and observed as several penguins swam in the water.

"Aren't they adorable?" Jada exclaimed enthusiastically.

"Yeah," Cutty replied. "Are they from South Africa?"

"They are," Jada responded. "They're not cold-climate birds, so the weather in Baltimore is agreeable to them. They're covered in tiny black and white feathers that help them stay warm and dry in the water. The color of the feathers helps them blend in with their environment. It's called countershading, and it's a form of camouflage," she added. "The black color on their backs helps them blend in with the water when they are viewed from above, whereas the white on their bellies helps them blend in when viewed from below. This helps the penguins hide from the fish they eat and from predators."

"That's incredible. Sounds like you've done your homework."

Jada smiled. After a while, the pair walked a short distance to watch some penguins on land. Four penguins stood on a log that protruded out of the water a little. Just before ten thirty, two zoo workers appeared on the land, each carrying a pail. The penguins rushed to their masters, who began to feed them fish.

"The penguins are fed twice per day, and the zoo-keepers keep track of how much they eat. This ensures each penguin receives the nutrition it requires while allowing the zookeepers to monitor their overall health."

Once again, Cutty seemed impressed by Jada's knowledge, and she caught him studying her casually as she watched the penguins.

Shortly, they continued their walk, passing some flamingos, ostriches, and tortoises. Next, they approached another watering hole, where the pair encountered some rhinoceroses, zebras, birds, and antelope. Then came the warthogs, cheetahs, and dik-diks, which were smaller species of antelope.

As they approached the giraffe area, Jada asked Cutty if he'd ever fed one before.

"Actually, no, I've never done that."

"Well, you are in for a treat today, Cutty." Jada purchased an acacia branch for three dollars and handed it to Cutty.

They stood on the other side of a fence as Cutty fed a young giraffe, holding out the branch as he'd been instructed while the animal nibbled it. The giraffe steadily ate until all the leaves had disappeared into its belly. Cutty let the remaining twig fall to the ground. All the while, Jada observed the wonderment in Cutty's eyes at such a task.

"That was cool." Cutty chuckled. "Thanks for the experience."

"My pleasure," she replied happily.

They continued walking until they reached the elephant landing, where they spent some time watching the elephants from the overlook. They passed some okapi, which were from the giraffe family and sported dark-chestnut coats with stripes on their hindquarters and upper legs. They continued slowly on their walk as they passed some lemurs, lions, crocodiles, and finally, some chimpanzees.

"This is the end of the African Journey. Are you ready for lunch?" Jada asked.

"I thought you'd never ask. I've been hungry ever since I fed that little giraffe." Cutty grinned.

Jada led the way to a vacant picnic table situated in a shady spot not too far from the food court. She opened her backpack and spread the contents on the table. "We have some chicken salad wraps, carrot sticks, and homemade chocolate chip cookies for dessert," she announced. "Help yourself."

They had already purchased water bottles when first entering the zoo. Jada set out some napkins, and the two quietly ate their meals while taking in their surroundings.

After eating his lunch and dessert, Cutty thanked Jada for the delicious meal.

"Aw, you're welcome. Aunt Ruby helped me. She's a fantastic cook."

"It's a wonder you don't weigh two hundred pounds," Cutty stated.

Jada rolled her eyes. They both used the nearby restrooms and decided to sit awhile under the shade of a large oak tree.

"Do you have any plans for summer vacation?" Jada asked.

"As a matter of fact, I do," Cutty replied. "I'll be spending two weeks with my parents. They live in Sneads Ferry, North Carolina."

"Did you grow up in North Carolina?" Jada asked.

"No, I grew up in Baltimore. My foster parents retired and moved to Sneads Ferry when I was halfway through college. It was their dream to move down South to be near their relatives. It's a beautiful area. I visit them every summer and sometimes during Christmas, and they visit me a couple of times a year. My dad takes me out shrimping on his brother's boat. It's pretty cool. Afterward, the women cook up a big meal of shrimp and salads. It's so good. I can hardly wait!"

"Sounds lovely," Jada stated. She noticed how Cutty's eyes lit up while talking about his family and the upcoming trip. She was truly happy for him. "When do you leave?"

"I leave this Saturday morning on the eight o'clock bus to North Carolina." Cutty gazed ahead as a group of children ran by, heading for the playground.

"Will the gym be closed while you're away?" Jada inquired.

"Not entirely. Some of the older boys, like Michael and Brodie, and my friends Levi and Elias will take turns supervising. It just won't be open all the usual hours I cover. But it'll be enough. Besides, it's prime holiday time, and some of the younger boys will be away visiting relatives and attending camps."

"Sounds like you have everything under control," Jada noted. "It's nice that the guys can cover for you. Do you pay them wages?"

"Yeah, I'm fortunate. I don't pay them, because they can use their time supervising at the gym as volunteer hours. The chiropractic office where I work part-time will be closed, too, so that's good."

"You work at a chiropractic office?" Jada was stunned.

"Yes. I work Thursday evenings there as a registered massage therapist. I pick up the occasional extra shift if I'm able to find a replacement at the gym."

"I had no idea. When did you take your training?"

"Shortly after I completed my education degree," Cutty answered. "I knew the chances of landing a teaching job were slim, and I'd always been interested in massage therapy and sports rehabilitation, so I enrolled in a massage therapy course. I recently completed the five hundred credit hours required and passed the MBLEx. That's the Massage & Bodywork Licensing Examination."

"Wow, congratulations! You are very ambitious." Jada was impressed.

Cutty smiled modestly. "How about you... any summer vacation plans?"

"Oh, yes. My aunt is taking Brodie and me to Disney World in Orlando. It's her high school graduation present to us. We leave on Saturday, August 2, and return one week later."

"That's right. I remember Brodie telling me about it. He won't be able to supervise at the gym during my second week away. Sounds exciting. I've never been there," Cutty added.

"Super exciting. And we're flying, so that's even better," Jada mentioned. She lay down on the grass, placing her head on top of her outstretched arm. Suddenly, she felt warm and tired. A small yawn escaped her. "Any word on the murdered boy's family?"

Cutty looked forward as he replied, "I know that Rev Joe planned on visiting the boy's family to see what he and his congregation can do for them. I need to touch base with the reverend. The thought of that boy, Devon, being shot at such a young age really haunts me."

"I know," Jada responded softly.

"It's senseless."

There was a brief pause but no response from Jada. Cutty turned and saw that Jada had fallen asleep. She looked so peaceful. Best to let her rest, as her body probably needed it.

Cutty stared ahead and watched as people passed. A few couples strolled by, holding hands. It reminded him of his last girlfriend, Tonya, whom he'd dated during their final year of education. It had been a casual kind of relationship, with no big plans for the future. She'd obtained a job across town at a high school upon graduation.

A couple of months into the fall teaching term, Tonya had abruptly ended their relationship after falling in love with a coworker. She had given Cutty his walking papers. He hadn't been too broken up about the situation. He'd only wished the best for Tonya. Besides, he'd been busy taking his massage therapy training and looking for jobs.

He'd been fortunate to find the position at the boxing gym a year and a half ago. It was a deacon at the church who had told Cutty about the opening. He'd known during the interview that it was where he was meant to be. The live-in suite attached to the gym was a bonus. He didn't own a car and had only a short commute to get to his massage therapy job once a week. *Things always have a way of working out for the best.*

Approximately twenty minutes later, some teenagers walked by, talking rather loudly.

Jada awoke with a start. "Did I fall asleep?"

"You sure did." Cutty turned to look at her.

"Sorry, I'm not being a very good tour guide." Jada sat up and brushed grass particles from her arm. "I had a busy day yesterday, helping Chloe clean her room. The heat made me drowsy."

"No worries," Cutty returned. "Do what you got to do. Besides, I enjoyed just sitting here, people watching." He grinned.

"That's good." Jada was glad. "Shall we see a few more animals before heading home?"

"Yeah, we might as well finish. Then we can check the Maryland Zoo off our to-do list for the summer," Cutty teased.

They stood and walked toward the Maryland Wilderness. Casually strolling through the farmyard, they saw cattle and goats taking shade under the trees. The train whistled in the distance as they passed through the meadow.

"I used to love riding the zoo train when I was a child. Aunt Ruby took Brodie and me during our summer holidays. She always let us ride the train. I can even remember my uncle Roy sitting with us. He enjoyed the train as much as we did. He passed away when Brodie and I were ten. He's probably watching us right now from heaven with a big smile on his face," Jada added.

"Sounds like he was a nice man," Cutty said thoughtfully. "Your aunt never met anyone else?"

"He was. And no, Aunt Ruby has stayed single all this time. She's devoted to Brodie and me, her job, church, and she loves quilting," Jada said. "It would be nice if she met someone, especially as Brodie and I will only be living at home for a few more years. And whoever it is would be one lucky man, since my aunt loves to cook!" Jada laughed.

"You'll have to send him over to the boxing gym to burn off the calories," Cutty added jovially.

The pair walked along the meadow and through the bat cave. They passed the bobcat area but didn't see any animals, as they were probably sleeping in shady, hidden spots. Next, they passed a stream, a marsh with birds, and finally, a bog. The temperature was a little cooler near the water areas, which the visitors welcomed.

"Well, that was a good depiction of the flora and fauna of Maryland," Jada said. "Let's just quickly stroll through the Polar Bear Watch, then we can head home."

"I'm in no rush," Cutty responded.

They encountered some bald eagles' nests high up in the trees as they made their way to the polar and grizzly bear pens. A few bears ambled around. Cutty and Jada stood awhile and watched the magnificent creatures.

"I wouldn't want to encounter a bear in the wilderness," Jada stated.

They passed by some arctic foxes and made their way to the walking path that led to the exit. Before they caught their bus, Cutty purchased another water bottle for each of them.

They were both fairly quiet on the bus ride home. Jada caught up on her texts while Cutty browsed Twitter. After the bus stopped near Jada's home, Cutty stood and let Jada exit first. They strolled to the front steps of the town house.

"I can't thank you enough for inviting me to the zoo today," Cutty said.

"Aw, I'm glad you came." Jada wrapped her arms around Cutty's waist and gave him a lingering hug.

"You're an amazing zoo guide." Cutty kissed the top of Jada's head as he returned the hug.

They slowly parted, and Cutty still held Jada's arms.

"Make sure to thank your aunt for the delicious lunch you two made." Cutty looked into Jada's eyes.

"Thanks, I will," Jada responded. "See you tomorrow." Jada walked up the steps to the front door. She unlocked it then turned to wave at Cutty.

"All right." Cutty turned and began his walk to the gym.

Chapter Five

THE FOLLOWING MORNING, JADA HEADED to the boxing gym for her usual workout. She'd had a good conversation with her aunt the previous evening, discussing the trip to the zoo and how it had seemed to brighten Cutty's demeanor.

"Why don't you invite Cutty to supper on Friday night, just before he heads south?" Ruby had suggested. "He'll be too busy packing after work to make a decent meal."

"Great idea," Jada had responded enthusiastically. She couldn't wait to ask him.

When Jada arrived at the gym, she was surprised to find Cutty was nowhere in sight. Instead, another man around Cutty's age appeared to be supervising the few boys in attendance that morning. Jada had seen the guy at the gym before. She just hadn't ever spoken to him.

"Hi, I'm Jada," she said, holding out her hand.

"Hey, the name's Levi," the man replied, shaking Jada's hand. "Cutty mentioned you might be working out this morning."

"Is he okay?" Jada asked.

"Yeah, he got called in to help with some patients at the chiropractic clinic. One of the staff is sick, so Cutty asked me to supervise." Levi seemed pleasant and charming.

Jada studied him, looking for signs of the addict Cutty had said he'd been. But there he stood, strong and clean with bright eyes filled with intelligence and kindness. He wasn't what Jada had expected of a former addict, but Cutty had said he'd turned his life around. Jada was glad Cutty and Elias had stood by him when he was down. Addiction didn't discriminate. It was an equal-opportunity destroyer.

"Cool. I'll just go about my routine and keep out of your way." Jada smiled.

"No worries. Take your time." Levi smiled back.

Before Jada began her workout, she sent Cutty a text inviting him to supper at her aunt's home on Friday evening. She figured he would be busy with patients, so she didn't expect him to reply right away. She put her earbuds in and listened to iTunes music while she exercised.

When her routine was complete, Jada walked over to Levi. "I'm gonna head home. Enjoy the rest of your day."

"Take care." Levi grinned as Jada turned and made her way to the exit.

Jada's phone vibrated on the desk, and her heart skipped a beat when she saw Cutty's name.

I can probably make it on Friday. Can I let you know for sure on Wednesday?

Jada's pulse quickened, and she did a little dance across her room with the phone clutched to her chest. *What is he doing to me?* All her thoughts somehow made their way back to Cutty, back to his smile, back to the way he was so patient with the boys as he wrapped their wrists.

She sat on her bed. *Wednesday is fine,* she typed and pressed send. She flopped back on her bed and let her thoughts fill with all things Cutty until Ruby called for dinner.

Jada sat with her aunt and watched some television prior to bed. "How is your quilt coming along?" she asked during the commercial break.

The work in progress sprawled across Ruby's lap as she carefully threaded a small needle with quilt thread. The coffee-table lamp had been repositioned to give ample lighting.

"Oh, fine," Aunt Ruby replied. "I plan on visiting the fabric store tomorrow, as I need a few more shades of green for the main pattern." After tying a knot, she inserted the needle between two layers of fabric and began to sew a straight line one quarter inch from the edge. Having done this for so many years, she didn't waste time drawing a pencil line first. She just eyeballed it.

"Who's it for?" Jada wondered if she would ever have the patience to learn the craft her aunt steadfastly practiced.

"Well, it's a gift," Aunt Ruby answered vaguely. "A little on the masculine side."

"He's a lucky guy, whoever it is!" Jada exclaimed.

They watched a little bit of the late news before retiring to bed.

Chloe met Jada for a walk the next morning, just before ten. "I have to work at noon," she said, leaning in for a hug.

"Cool. You ready for school?" Jada asked.

Chloe would be starting nursing school that fall.

"Yeah. I get to tour the clinic next week, so I'll be able to get some answers then."

"That's good," Jada noted. "The first semester will be here before we know it."

"For sure," Chloe agreed. "How about you? Are things lining up?"

"Yeah. The rec center's holding a meet and greet this Friday for the men's basketball team and my squad."

"Aw, fun!" Chloe stated. "Watch out for those jocks."

Jada giggled at her friend's comment. "I wish you were coming with me. How will we ever survive without one another?"

"We'll manage, somehow. We'll just have to plan some shopping dates. We have to look good, after all," Chloe remarked.

"Absolutely," Jada responded.

The two girls walked past the Lutheran church, where the reverend worked. The old Suburban was parked beside a few cars in the parking lot.

"How was your trip to the zoo with Cutty?"

"We had a great time. He's just so calm. Like I totally fell asleep after we ate lunch, and he just let me do it. Said that he people watched. It was a good day." Jada smiled, remembering. "He needed it after finding out about that kid who got shot. Devon Lewis, that was his name. I don't think Cutty knew him, but it really affected him. He's got a good heart. I think the zoo took his mind off everything else, you know?"

"And it did the trick?" Chloe probed.

"I think so. I bought an acacia branch so he could feed it to a giraffe. He'd never done that before. He looked like a kid, his eyes full of wonder."

"Aw, I bet he enjoyed that."

"Yeah, he sure did," Jada said. "Anyways, he mentioned that Rev Joe would be in touch with Devon's family. I think Cutty plans on helping out in some way, if possible."

"Well, that's very good of him. We've got to send prayers for Devon's family and friends," Chloe added. "And the Baltimore City Police, so they can catch the perpetrators."

"Amen," Jada concluded. "How is Michael's job hunt?"

"Decent," Chloe replied. "He may have found a part-time job that would fulfill his apprenticeship hour requirements. So it looks like he'll be joining Brodie at the technical college this fall."

"Right on!" Jada exclaimed. "He must be so relieved."

"Yeah," Chloe confirmed.

The girls parted ways at the Smith residence so Chloe could get ready for work. Once Jada arrived home, she placed her laptop on the living room floor, spread out her mat, and did a hatha yoga practice off YouTube.

Jada felt anticipation as she headed to the gym on Wednesday morning. She hoped Cutty would be able to join them for supper on Friday so she could spend more time with him away from the gym.

A new notice hung on the bulletin board advertising mouth guards for boxers and weight lifters. A local dental clinic was offering them to gym members at a discount. Cutty approached Jada as she read the poster.

"Good morning, shawty." Cutty smiled as he gently touched Jada's arm.

"Hi, stranger," Jada replied. "Do I need one of these mouth guards?" She pointed at the poster.

"They're really more for the boxers than the weight lifters. The mouth guard protects the teeth as well as stabilizes the jaw. So if a boxer is hit in the jaw, the neck and skull are stabilized because the guard keeps the jaw in place. Without it, a punch with enough force could knock out your teeth. Beyond that, it prevents brain injuries. Also, wearing a mouth guard toughens up a boxer's mental thinking."

"Well done. You always look out for the boys' well-being." Jada couldn't help but notice the spark was back in Cutty's eyes.

"Thanks." Cutty paused briefly. "And I can make it to dinner on Friday, if the invitation still stands."

"Oh, yes. Aunt Ruby will be pleased. How does five thirty sound?"

"That sounds perfect. I won't stay too late, as I'll be meeting the boys for a drink then calling it a night before my trip."

"No problem… as long as you stay for Aunt Ruby's dessert," Jada added.

"Noted," Cutty replied.

"Okay, I better get moving." Jada headed toward the cardio equipment.

She caught Cutty gazing at her for a moment from the corner of her eye as she walked away.

About ninety minutes later, Jada found Cutty ring-side watching some boxers.

"I'll see you Friday at supper?"

"All right." Cutty thought for a moment. "Won't you be at the gym on Friday morning?"

"Nah, I promised to help Aunty on Friday morning, then I have to go to the university in the afternoon."

"All right, Friday evening it is, then. I'm really look-ing forward to it." Cutty grinned.

"Great. I think she's inviting Rev Joe also."

"Awesome," Cutty said happily.

"Bye." Jada slowly turned.

"See ya." Cutty nodded at her.

By Friday morning, Cutty was mostly packed for his trip to see his parents. He had kept up with his laundry all week, as his suite was equipped with a stackable washer and dryer. His shift at the chiropractic office the previous evening had flown by. Cutty was looking forward to dinner at Jada's. He had a feeling that Ruby would be barbecuing something delicious. He also looked forward to seeing the reverend. He always enjoyed his visits with Rev Joe.

Only a few boys were at the gym, so Cutty had time to run through the gym's supervision schedule and hours of operation for when he was away. He texted all parties involved one final time to make sure they knew the plan. He felt privileged to be able to visit with his folks while his friends minded the gym. It also made Cutty feel better knowing the gym would be available, albeit on a lighter schedule, for the kids who didn't have an opportunity to get away for the summer.

It seemed a little odd not having Jada working out that morning. Cutty had enjoyed getting to know her better. She was easy to talk to, bright, and quite mature for her age.

Cutty closed the gym at four thirty so he had time to shower before supper. The few boys leaving at the end wished Cutty a nice holiday. On his way to the Parkers' town house, he made a slight diversion from his usual route to buy a bouquet of flowers for Ruby. He made the purchase at a small corner store, one block north of the gym. At five thirty, Cutty rang the Parkers' doorbell.

Brodie opened the door. "Hey, Cutty." Brodie stepped aside to let his guest pass.

"Hello, Brodie."

The guys fist-bumped.

"I hope you brought an appetite. Mom's been cooking up a storm."

"I sure did," Cutty replied. He saw Rev Joe sitting in the living room. "Evening, Reverend." Cutty nodded his way.

"Hello, Cutty. Nice to see you," the reverend responded.

"Hello, Mrs. Par—Ruby." Cutty remembered her previous invitation to call her by her Christian name.

"Welcome, Cutty. It's always a pleasure to see you. Make yourself at home. Brodie, can you offer him a drink, please?" Ruby was finishing the supper preparations in the kitchen.

"Absolutely. What'll you have, Cutty? Water, iced tea, milk?" Brodie listed.

Cutty noticed that the reverend was drinking iced tea. "I'll have what the reverend is having, please." He followed Brodie into the kitchen and handed Ruby the modest bouquet of flowers.

"Why, Cutty, you shouldn't have," Ruby said. "They are just lovely. Thank you. I have the perfect vase for them." Ruby reached for a clear vase above the fridge.

"It's my pleasure, ma'am. I've been looking forward to this supper since Monday. Where is Jada, by the way?" Cutty took the glass of iced tea from Brodie. "Thanks." Cutty raised his glass to his friend.

"She attended a meet and greet at the university today for the cheerleaders and the men's basketball team. She just texted me that it ran over the scheduled time, and she'll be home for supper a little later than expected," Ruby replied.

"Hmm," Cutty uttered, mildly disappointed. He watched as Ruby added water to the vase from the kitchen tap and placed the flowers in it. The bouquet consisted of three white Asiatic lilies, some blue hydrangeas, and raspberry *sinuata statice* arranged with lemon leaf and spiral eucalyptus.

"Brodie, would you mind putting the steaks on the grill now, please?" After placing the vase on top of the kitchen island, Ruby handed Brodie a dish of steaks in a marinade.

"Sure thing." Brodie took the dish from his mom and headed toward the backyard deck.

Cutty sat down on a couch, near the reverend. "How's your week been, Rev Joe?"

"Fairly decent. I reached out to the Lewis family."

"How did that go?"

"As well as one can expect under the circumstances. I met Devon's mother, Clarice—she's a single mom and works at the nursing home—and Devon's younger brother, Davey. He's coming on thirteen. They've taken Devon's loss very hard. It seems that Devon was trying to earn some extra income for the household to help his mom out with the bills and all, but he chose an unfortunate path. Got sucked in by the drug gang," the reverend reflected. "The police are still sorting out the details. No one seems to want to talk, in case of retribution."

"That doesn't surprise me one bit," Cutty commented, shaking his head. "The Baltimore City Police will have their work cut out for them. I wonder if they have any informants."

"Good question," the reverend responded. "I pray that they take it seriously and push forward, given the young age of their victim."

"I sure hope so," Cutty added. "The kids need some reassurance that they will be safe on the streets. It's such a bad deal for everyone."

"I've mentioned the incident during my sermons the past two Sundays. Some of my parishioners have volunteered to make meals for Devon's family and to do stuff around their town house as needed."

"That's good to hear," Cutty said. "Actually, it warms the heart a little, all things considered."

"Yes, we at St. Peter's are highly favored by God." The reverend nodded. "And we want to reap what we sow."

He and Cutty spent a few minutes discussing the schedule at the gym for when Cutty was on holidays and what some of the young boxing members would be up to for the summer.

Before long, Ruby announced that the steaks were ready and invited the men to the table. Cutty and Rev Joe made their way to the nicely set table.

Before they sat, the reverend asked, "Shall we wait for Jada, Ruby?"

"No. She texted that there's a traffic jam and the bus she's on is sitting still at the moment. She sends her apologies and said to begin supper without her." Ruby placed some bowls laden with food on the table, then she and Brodie sat down as well. "Will you do the honors and say Grace?" Ruby looked at Rev Joe.

"Absolutely," the reverend replied confidently, and everyone bowed their head. "Heavenly Father, we are so blessed to be in Your presence on this fine summer evening. We ask that You bless this food we are about to eat, prepared by our gracious host, Ruby, and her family. We ask You to deliver Jada home safely and to be with Cutty, Father, as he journeys to Sneads Ferry tomorrow to visit his parents. We ask these things in Your name, Dear Father. In Jesus's name, we pray. Amen."

"Amen," the other three replied.

"Thank you, Reverend." Ruby smiled.

She offered Cutty the platter of steaks first. Brodie followed suit and passed the reverend a large bowl filled to the brim with potato salad.

Just then, the front door flew open, and in walked Jada. Everyone stared up at her as she entered.

"Sorry for being late!" Jada was flushed.

"No worries, child," the reverend said. "We are just thankful you made it home safe and that you get to join us for this lovely meal."

"Okay, thank you, Reverend. I'll just freshen up and join you. Please continue eating." Jada looked helplessly at Cutty.

Cutty, in turn, stared back. He had never seen Jada with her hair down before. Her tresses were beautiful—long and shiny black with a few large waves. And her dress looked utterly stunning on her. It was a short orange halter dress that featured vertical pleats. She wore large gold hoop earrings and shimmery gold wedge-heeled sandals. *She's a showstopper tonight.*

Jada ran upstairs as the others continued passing the dishes around and filling their plates with the food.

"This is such a treat for us bachelors," the reverend said.

A few minutes later, Jada returned from upstairs and joined them at the table. Her aunt and cousin passed her the dishes of food, and she was almost set to eat. She quickly bowed her head and gave a silent prayer as Brodie stood to get Jada a glass of iced tea.

"Here. This will cool you off some."

"Thank you, Brodie. Looks like the steaks turned out nice," Jada commented.

"The meat is delicious," the reverend added.

"It's all in my mom's secret marinade." Brodie grinned.

"It's no secret," Ruby replied. "But it sure tenderizes the meat and gives it flavor."

"This potato salad is incredible. In fact, I think it's about the best I've ever had." Cutty finally found his voice after being so mesmerized by Jada's appearance.

"Well, we have to give Jada all the credit for it. She made it this morning, and let me tell you, potato salad can be very time-consuming," Ruby announced.

"Is that so?" Cutty looked across the table at Jada.

"Thank you, and yes, I made it. But it's my aunt's recipe. It's been in the family for years." Jada smiled, settling into the group and hydrating, thanks to Brodie, as she seemed to get over her initial embarrassment. "But I have one secret ingredient—besides love, that is."

"And what would that be?" Cutty inquired.

"It's mustard, believe it or not. You add just the slightest amount when you mix the mayonnaise with the salt and pepper. It gives the potato salad a nice flavor," Jada shared.

"That's the reason you missed your workout this morning?" Cutty teased.

"Yes, as a matter of fact, it is," Jada responded proudly.

"Well then, as supervisor of the gym, I approve." Cutty grinned.

The dinner companions continued eating. In addition to barbecued steaks and potato salad, Ruby had also prepared green beans, a gelatin salad, and some home-made biscuits for her guests. Fortunately, Ruby had installed air-conditioning in her townhome a few years prior, so the temperature inside was comfortable.

The reverend asked Cutty about his vacation plans while visiting his parents in Sneads Ferry, and Cutty was happy to share the details. Besides spending time with his parents, whom he adored, Cutty looked forward to running along the beach and paths near the estuary in the mornings. Then there was the fishing and eating. It was always such a pleasant trip for Cutty, and he looked forward to it.

After everyone had finished eating, Ruby and Jada cleared the dinner plates and put the leftover food away. Ruby put a kettle of water on to make some decaffeinated tea. Then she brought dessert out from the refrigerator.

"I hope you all saved room for some of Aunt Ruby's dessert," Jada said.

"What has Ruby created this time?" the reverend asked, his interest piqued.

"Blueberry-cheesecake crumb cake," Jada answered. "It's the pièce de résistance."

Cutty perked up at this disclosure. "Count me in."

"Me also, but not too big of a piece. I don't work out like you three young people do," the reverend proclaimed, patting his stomach a little.

Ruby cut five pieces of blueberry cheesecake, and Jada served the dessert to the men. The reverend and

Ruby sipped on some tea. As they sat around the table, the reverend asked Brodie how his new job was going.

"Quite well," Brodie replied. "So far, I've been working in the shipping and receiving department so I'm able to learn about all the parts the electrical and plumbing company supplies. It'll be good background information for when I start trade school in the fall."

"Excellent." The reverend was genuine in his response. "Your mom tells me you helped Michael secure a position as well."

"Yes, indeed. My boss was kind enough to arrange that with a competitor. But in this business, they try and help one another out," Brodie explained.

"Good work. I'll bet Michael is relieved," Cutty added.

"Yeah, he's pumped," Brodie responded. "Looks like I'll have a study buddy for the fall."

Everyone laughed at this.

Cutty stood and placed his plate on the counter near the kitchen sink. "I'll be off now, if you all don't mind. I'm meeting Elias and Levi for a drink."

Everyone stood.

"No worries, Cutty," Ruby said. "Have a nice time with your friends and a wonderful visit with your folks." She gave Cutty a hug.

"Thank you, Ruby. The supper was divine," Cutty stated emphatically.

"Blessings, Cutty. Enjoy your time. You've earned it." The reverend shook Cutty's hand.

"Well, when I turn twenty-one, I'll be able to join you at the bar!" Brodie hugged Cutty.

"Thanks for supervising at the gym, Brodie. And have a great time in Disney World," Cutty replied.

"I'll try. Oh, can I just show you my mouth guard quickly?" Brodie grabbed a small case off the island. He opened it and took out a clear, custom-fit mouth guard.

"You had one made already?" Cutty was astonished.

"Yeah, I stopped in at the dental office yesterday after work to make an appointment. Turned out they had time to take the impression right then. They called me this afternoon to let me know it was ready, so I picked it up on my way home from work."

"Very nice. How's the fit?" Cutty asked.

"It's good. They had limited colors to choose from, so I picked clear. Apparently, boxers shouldn't wear red or orange mouth guards because they could look like blood and that could confuse a referee."

"The dentist told me that when I consulted with him about making the boys' mouth guards. That's interesting. You'll have to show the boys when you're supervising next week. It'll be a good reminder for them to make their appointments." Cutty started walking toward the front door.

Jada followed him. "I'll walk you home, Cutty, if you don't mind."

"Not at all," Cutty answered. "Unless you're tired."

"It's all good. Besides, I won't see you for two weeks," Jada reminded him as they walked down the steps and along the sidewalk.

Having crossed the first street, they strolled about ten feet, then Jada tucked her hand into Cutty's elbow. "I'll just hold on to you if that's okay. These heels are slowing me down. I should have put on some flats."

"Fine by me," Cutty acknowledged. "You look very beautiful tonight."

"Thank you." Jada blushed.

They walked in silence for a couple of minutes then crossed the second street.

"How did your event go today?" Cutty probed.

"It went well. I got to meet most of the cheerleading squad. Two girls were away on holiday. But they all seem very nice." Jada paused. "One of the girls I met will be in most of my classes the first semester. Her name is Olivia. We exchanged cell numbers."

"Oh, that's reassuring," Cutty noted. "And how were the basketball players?"

Jada chuckled. "Well, from what I could tell, they seem very polite, if not a little shy."

"Really?" Cutty was surprised. "I would have thought they'd be all over your squad."

"Not today," Jada reaffirmed. "They were too busy dribbling their basketballs."

They crossed the third street.

As they neared the entrance to the boxing gym, Jada changed the topic. "I am going to miss you,

62

Cutty. Working out just won't be the same without you around." She smiled up at Cutty as he stood facing her. "Have a really nice time visiting your family. Promise you'll be safe, especially when you're on the boat?"

"I promise, Jada. We wear life jackets, if that eases your mind." Cutty looked reassuringly down into Jada's eyes.

Jada placed her hands on Cutty's chest. Then, she leaned up and planted a kiss on his lips.

Cutty was pleasantly surprised. He didn't back away too quickly. When he did, he stared deeply at Jada. Their demeanor grew more serious, more intense. Suddenly, Cutty cupped the back of Jada's head with one hand while placing the other on top of her collarbone. With one fluid movement, Cutty carefully leaned Jada against the inside wall of the doorway. He kissed her passionately, if not forcefully. He skillfully searched Jada's mouth with his tongue, and she responded in kind. His hand began softly massaging Jada's neck then ran down the center of her dress. He fanned his fingers out above her waist while his thumb grazed the lower part of her breast. His hand came to rest on Jada's lower back as he leaned into her body.

When they finally broke apart, Jada was breathless.

Cutty didn't know what had possessed him. In part, it had something to do with the way Jada looked tonight. Stunning. But also, it had to do with the fact that she would be socializing with other young men at college. Cutty felt a desire to lay claim to Jada, even if he didn't have a right to.

After he caught his breath, Cutty spoke in a low tone. "You better get yourself home, or neither one of us will be safe." His eyes implored her.

Jada nodded then backed away. She turned and walked down the sidewalk, careful to not trip in her wedge sandals.

Cutty stood, one arm leaning against the outside wall of the gym, and watched Jada depart. Part of him wanted to escort her safely home, tell her endearments. But the rational part told Cutty to stay put. He'd made his mark.

Chapter Six

PART OF JADA DIDN'T WANT to leave that night after their kiss, while the other part sought solitude to relive the kiss in its entirety. And when she got home, it continued to play in her mind until she climbed into bed.

Not only did Jada have a solid sleep, she slept in for the first time in a long while. Her alarm clock read 9:40 a.m. She thought about Cutty sitting on a bus somewhere, heading for North Carolina. She replayed the kiss from the previous evening over and over in her mind. She couldn't help but smile dreamily. *How on earth am I going to manage two weeks without seeing him?*

For starters, she'd better get her butt out of bed and start moving, especially since she missed her workout the previous day. Making the potato salad had been a labor of love. And Cutty had paid her the highest of compliments. The whole meal was delicious, especially the blueberry-cheesecake crumb cake. She felt fortunate not only to have the most caring aunt as her guardian but also the best cook. They would just have to invite Cutty over more often, starting when they returned from their summer holidays.

Jada turned on her iPhone. Cutty had sent her a text at 7:45 a.m. She held her breath then opened his message. *Thanks again for supper. I hope I didn't scare you off last night.*

She sighed a breath of relief and replied, *My pleasure, all good*, along with a kissy-face emoji. It was more than good. *I hope you had fun with the boys!*

Jada sent Chloe a text, *Wanna work out today?* She needed some girl time.

How about two-ish? Chloe replied.

Sure. It was perfect timing, since they had plans to go bowling with Brodie and Michael in the evening.

After eating breakfast, Jada checked in on her aunt in the basement. Ruby was working on the quilt, which was spread taut over a wooden frame. She was quite content in her bubble, listening to her favorite radio talk show. Jada leaned over and gave her aunt a hug.

"How did you sleep, Jada?"

"Like a baby, I suppose. I don't remember the last time I slept in."

"Well, you've spent the past twelve years having to get up early for school. It gets ingrained in one's internal clock. I would know... up every morning with the chickens." Ruby sighed. She was usually awake by six.

"How big is this quilt going to be?"

"It's for a queen-size bed," Ruby answered.

"So not meant for Brodie's or my room, then," Jada said curiously.

She and her cousin each had a double bed.

"I reckon not. Unless either of you are planning to move out and buy bigger beds," Ruby responded, chuckling. "The dinner turned out well last night," she said to change the subject.

"It was so good, Aunty. Your dessert was a hit. Where did you find the recipe?"

"I saw it on Facebook. The picture looked good, so I took a chance and gave it a try."

"Well, good thing. Cutty really liked it," Jada reminisced.

"Yes, it appeared so. But not as much as he enjoyed your potato salad." It was Ruby's turn to be inquisitive.

"Yeah, he was so sweet." Jada smiled. "I'm so glad he could join us for supper and still go out with his friends. It won't be the same without him at the gym."

"Remember, it's only one week until we fly to Orlando," Ruby stated. "You and Brodie will get plenty of exercise there, walking around the big park, chasing Mickey."

"You're right. Have you ever flown in a plane?"

"Once, before I had Brodie. Your uncle Roy and I went to a longshoreman convention in San Diego. The union paid for Roy and me to fly to California." The same union had also provided Ruby with a pension since she'd become a widow.

"Aw, nice. Were there palm trees everywhere?" Jada asked.

"Yes. Palm trees, ocean, and quite a military presence. San Diego is the second largest surface ship base of the United States Navy. Roy was fascinated with it all."

"Cool," Jada responded. "I just told Cutty about Uncle Roy last Sunday, how he used to love taking Brodie and me on the train at the zoo."

"Did you, now?" Ruby seemed pleasantly surprised.

"Yeah. I miss Uncle Roy. He was a good man."

"He sure was. Proverbs 10:7 tells us that 'good people will be remembered as a blessing.' I miss my Roy also." The women took a brief, reflective pause.

"Aunty, can we invite Cutty over for supper again when we return from our holiday?"

"Well, sure," Ruby replied. "He's an easy guest to have. And he does a lot for our community. Rev Joe speaks highly of him."

Jada was pleased at the news. She told her aunt about her plans with Chloe for the afternoon and evening. Then she took her leave.

"Nice form!" Jada complimented Chloe as she executed a barbell bench press loaded with fifty pounds. She had a slight arch in her lower back. She drove the bar upward while keeping her torso and legs tight. Jada stood behind the bench, spotting as Chloe placed the bar back on the J-hooks with a loud clang.

"The girl's got stamina!" Brodie exclaimed as he walked by. He had his iTunes cranked up.

After wiping the sweat off her forehead with a towel, Chloe took a sip of water. "What's next?"

"How about some lat pull-downs?" Jada suggested. It was chest and back day for her, and Chloe was down for it. "Wanna start with seventy pounds?"

"Sure." Chloe watched as Jada loaded the plates on each side of the multi-gym. Jada began the set.

When it was Chloe's turn, Brodie hovered nearby. "You can lean back a little once the weights get heavier," he suggested.

Jada loaded ten more pounds on each side for their second set.

"How much heavier are we talkin'?" Chloe looked flushed.

"You got this," Brodie encouraged.

Chloe managed to complete her reps after Jada's turn.

"Let's do some stretches now." Jada grabbed two mats lined up along the wall and placed them parallel to each other, leaving some room between them.

"Cutty and I had our first kiss last night," she shared as soon as Brodie was out of earshot.

"Ohhhh!" Chloe gushed. "Do tell."

The girls sat down on the mats, facing each other.

"I walked him to the gym after supper. I actually instigated it, but he—" Jada quickly clamped her mouth shut as Brodie reappeared. "Don't you have some boxers to supervise?" she admonished.

"Ouch, cuz." Brodie feigned a hurt face and walked away.

"He what?" Chloe sought more.

"Well, I wasn't sure if he would be... receptive... but—" Jada blushed as she paused her story.

"But?" Chloe pressed.

"He was," Jada continued. "Very receptive, I mean." She ginned full-on, remembering how it took her breath away.

"Sweet," Chloe responded. "Too bad he's gone now." She lowered her voice as a couple of boys walked by. "Girl, you're moving into new territory."

"Tell me about it." Jada sighed as she moved into a seated yoga twist.

"Just don't be too eager, you know?" Chloe suggested.

"What do you mean?" Jada inquired.

"I mean, now that Cutty's away, don't be texting him every day," Chloe instructed confidently. "Let him miss you, seek you out."

"Ah, good point." Jada got the message. *How did Chloe suddenly become the dating expert?*

Later that evening, Michael and Chloe pulled up outside the Parkers' home in their dad's 2006 white Honda Accord. Brodie and Jada jumped into the back seat of the car.

"Can you turn up the volume?" Brodie requested. "I dig this song."

"Sure." Chloe did the honors so Michael could focus on driving while Brodie sang in tune to the hip-hop beat. Traffic moved along steadily as they headed toward the bowling alley.

No parking spaces were available near the venue, so Michael ended up parking a few blocks away.

"These buildings look abandoned," Jada said as they began their trek.

The dilapidated structures lining the streets were missing their windows, not a shard of glass to be seen.

"Looks like garbage piled up inside this one," Chloe added.

Trash lay strewn about the sidewalk, with grass and weeds sprouting up everywhere. It could have been a pasture, save for all the cracked concrete that was once well-trodden. It felt as though they were walking through a ghost town.

"You got any spare change, kid?" a disheveled older man asked Michael.

"No," Michael responded adamantly.

He didn't like to part with his money, especially when he was caught off guard, Jada knew.

"Well, you're sure sportin' some fancy shoes," the stranger persisted, pointing at Michael's Nike high-top sneakers.

"Yeah, I worked hard for these shoes." Michael wasn't backing down.

"Here you go." Brodie thrust a ten-dollar bill into the man's hand and gave him a pat on the arm. "Have a good evening." Brodie walked toward the venue. "C'mon." He encouraged his companions to follow.

"He worked hard for his shoes," the man mumbled. The ragged sandals he wore had seen better days.

"Why'd you do that?" Michael asked his friend in surprise once they were out of earshot.

"Look, the last thing we need is trouble. Let's just get our butts to the bowling alley," Brodie replied.

"You know he's probably just gonna spend that money on drugs, right?" Michael shook his head.

"I dunno." Brodie shrugged.

The girls steered clear of the topic.

Once the foursome reached their destination, they rented shoes and paid for two games of bowling. They were fortunate to get a lane, as the place got busier after they began playing.

Brodie won the first game, scoring eighty-eight points. He was lucky enough to get a strike early in the game. Chloe won the second game, scoring seventy-nine points. She managed to get a spare near the end. All four of them threw their share of gutter balls.

Afterward, the group split some nachos from the snack bar.

"Has anyone heard from Cutty?" Michael asked.

"Yeah, as a matter of fact, he recently texted that he arrived at Sneads Ferry. Long bus ride, though." Brodie looked at his iPhone. "I wouldn't wanna do it." He shook his head. "Cutty asked me how things went at the gym today."

With the new information, Jada perked up, receiving a knowing look from Chloe.

"I'll be supervising at the gym on Tuesday," Michael announced. "And Levi will be there on Monday."

"Aw, he's so nice," Jada chimed in. "Does he work?"

"Yeah, part-time in harm reduction," Michael informed. "I think he goes to school too."

"That's right. He's takin' psychology," Brodie added. "Matter of fact, he goes to the University of Baltimore." He looked in Jada's direction.

"Cool." Jada looked forward to seeing Levi on Monday, knowing they had school in common.

"When will you be supervising next?" Chloe asked Brodie.

"I'll be at the gym Wednesday and Thursday evenings, after my job ends for the day. I saved Friday night for packing. Then my mom, Jada, and I leave for Orlando on Saturday."

"You guys are so lucky," Michael stated. "I'd love to go there someday."

"We should plan a trip for when we all finish school," Chloe added, looking at Brodie.

"Sounds good." Brodie winked in reply.

"I'm in. Are you guys about ready to leave?" Michael asked.

"Sure." Jada stood and placed the empty food containers in a nearby garbage bin. They all headed toward the door.

Mindful of their surroundings, they made their way to the car. The vibe had shifted as more people loitered about the streets. Shouting could be heard in the distance. The rule of thumb was safety in numbers.

When they reached the car, Brodie walked to the front passenger door to open it for Chloe. "Oh man! Was this scratch here before?" he exclaimed.

"Get out," Michael said in disbelief, walking toward Brodie and observing the front door. "Nope. That was done tonight, while we were inside the bowling alley." Someone had keyed his dad's Accord, making about a twelve-inch scratch close to the door handle.

"Rats," Chloe responded. "It's not your fault, Michael. Or any of ours. Dad's going to be disappointed. But at least it's not a brand-new car."

"This is the last thing I need." Michael sighed, disheartened. He took a picture of the car door on his iPhone and sent it to his dad along with a text message about what had happened.

"Unfortunately, bad stuff happens everywhere," Jada added.

They all got into the vehicle, and Michael headed toward the Parkers' home. Michael and Brodie chatted a little about Michael's new job that he would be starting part-time on Monday.

Once Michael pulled up to the town house, Jada and Brodie thanked their friends for the nice evening as well as the ride. Everyone except Michael got out of the car. Jada gave Chloe a brief hug. As Jada turned to walk toward the front steps, she noticed Chloe and Brodie exchange a hug out of the corner of her eye. *That's odd.* She didn't recall those two ever being close or touchy-feely toward one another.

The following week was fairly uneventful. Jada stayed true to her exercise schedule and enjoyed chatting with Levi on Monday. His goal was to work with people in need and possibly pursue a career in counseling.

By Friday evening, Jada, Brodie, and Ruby were packed and ready for their trip to Disney World the following morning. Jada and her aunt watched a movie before retiring to bed. It helped them wind down so they could hopefully get a good night's rest. Brodie got ready to leave and told the girls he had to head over to Michael's for a bit.

"As long as you don't miss your flight," his mom chided.

"I wouldn't miss the flight for the world." Brodie chuckled. "Pardon the pun!" And out the door he went, grinning.

Chapter Seven

C UTTY EXHALED WHILE LIFTING THE bar for a shoulder press. He was using the Smith Machine at the boxing gym, having arrived home from North Carolina the night before. He'd done a fair bit of running and walking while visiting his folks in Sneads Ferry, and he'd even managed to drop into a local gym a few times. But nothing beat working out at his own gym. It helped him get over the fatigue of the long bus ride home and saying goodbye to his family.

He was listening to a song by the Weeknd on iTunes and was quite interested in the music by Abel Tesfaye, who grew up in Toronto, Canada. The lyrics sung by the new artist were explicit, but the singer had a unique voice. Cutty was careful not to expose the music to the younger boys at the gym, hence his earbuds. The music energized him to lift. And lift he did that morning.

Cutty practiced what he preached. And that was proper breathing during weight lifting, which was vital for one's performance and health. Breathing ensured the blood circulating to the muscles was oxygenated and that waste products were removed. Holding one's breath during weight lifting could lead to increased blood pressure, fatigue, and dizziness, which could result in injury.

He taught the kids in his gym to start lifting with light weights until breathing correctly became second nature, as heavy weights demanded more concentration and strength, which made it easier to forget to breathe properly.

Another breath in as Cutty lowered the bar to chest height, finishing the set. He was suddenly aware of someone in his field of vision as he racked the bar. Turning his head slightly, he was pleasantly surprised to see Jada's smiling face. "Oh, hey." He removed his earbuds as he stood.

"Hello, stranger." Jada was quick to wrap her arms around Cutty's waist and give him a welcoming hug.

Cutty hugged her in return, giving her back a slight rub with his right hand. When they parted, he took a step back. "Look at you, all pretty in pink." Cutty eyed Jada's new workout attire. He was used to hanging out with sweaty boys most of the time.

"Thanks. I bought this at Lululemon in Orlando." Jada wore a baby-pink halter top with a matching strappy sports bra. The straps fanned out over her upper back and added a soft, feminine look. She paired the set with some black cropped leggings from her closet.

"Very nice. Is that an athletic store?" Cutty asked.

"Actually, it's a yoga-inspired store for men and women. It originated in Vancouver, Canada, in 1998."

"You've been doing your research again." Cutty chuckled.

"Google." Jada grinned up at Cutty. "How've you been? How was the visit with your parents?"

"I'm tired from the bus ride yesterday. But the visit was amazing." Cutty beamed. "My parents are great, just getting a little older. The weather cooperated, for the most part. And the food was fantastic." Cutty patted his stomach. "That's why I'm working out this morning. Got a little soft around the middle."

"Oh, I hear you," Jada agreed. "We did our share of walking in Orlando. My feet are still a little sore, but Brodie and I didn't make it to the gym. We didn't have time. Thankfully, we managed to jump into the hotel pool a couple of times. It was so hot."

"I see. So, Disney World was good to you?"

"Very good," Jada replied. "Brodie and I had so much fun. Aunt Ruby took lots of breaks. She'd sit and people watch while Brodie and I stood in line for the rides. We used some Fast Passes. Oh, and did you know that some of the lines have a water mist that sprays people to cool them down while they wait?"

"I didn't know that." Cutty was taken with Jada's enthusiasm. "But that makes sense. Probably prevents some people from fainting of heat exhaustion."

"Good point. Not so great for the hair, though."

"And you managed to get in some shopping?" Cutty probed.

"We sure did," Jada answered happily. "I got a little something for you too." Jada handed Cutty a small red-and-white reusable shopping bag with handles, black trim, and the Lululemon Athletica logo on it. "I used money from graduation gifts to splurge on my shopping spree."

"Oh. You didn't have to do that," Cutty exclaimed. He opened the bag and pulled out a berry-colored fitted T-shirt. "This is great—so nice of you, Jada." He held the shirt up and placed it close to his chest.

"I think it should fit you. Brodie helped me with the size," Jada informed him.

"I'm sure it's perfect. Thank you." Cutty looked at Jada. "I wasn't expecting anything."

"Well, I could have brought back some Mickey Mouse ears for you," Jada teased.

Cutty laughed.

"Did everyone here at the gym survive?" Jada asked.

"I think so. At least, I didn't receive any strange texts while I was away. Nor has any parent yet to complain, so fingers crossed." Cutty placed the T-shirt back in its bag.

"That must be a relief."

"Yeah, for sure. Are you doing your usual routine?"

"Yeah. Right away," Jada answered. "I was hoping you could come over for supper tonight."

"Oh… well. I don't want to bother your aunt." Cutty was a little caught off guard.

"Trust me, you're no bother. It'll be fairly simple tonight—hamburgers, actually," Jada persisted. "We've been home since early Saturday afternoon. Aunt Ruby and I went grocery shopping yesterday, so things are fairly under control." Jada gave Cutty a cajoling look. "And Aunt Ruby and I would love to hear about your holiday."

"Well, I suppose… Can I bring anything?"

"Just yourself," Jada reassured him. "Can you make it for six?"

"Yeah." Cutty nodded. "That could work."

"Great! I better start my workout. It's nice seeing you again." Jada smiled.

"All right, then. It's good to be back, Jada."

On her way home from the gym, Jada stopped at the closest grocery store and purchased some ice cream for dessert. It felt good to have the workout under her belt and to see Cutty. Their encounter had gone well, not awkward at all. It gave her a warm feeling.

Once home, Jada placed the ice cream inside the freezer and fixed herself some lunch. Then she went downstairs to the sewing room to visit her aunt. Ruby was working on her quilting project again.

"Looks like you're making up for lost time," Jada stated.

"Yeah, I missed it. Won't be long until I'm back at work." Ruby was a secretary at the elementary school Brodie and Jada had attended. "Then I'll have less time for sewing."

"Aw. Well, I have good news. Cutty agreed to come over for supper tonight," Jada said ardently.

"Oh, that's good. Did he have a nice visit with his folks?"

"Yeah, sounds like it. He was worried about being a burden to you, Aunty. But I assured him that it was no trouble and that we wanted to hear all about his vacation. I bought some ice cream on my way home."

"Lovely," Ruby responded to the enthusiasm evident in Jada's voice.

The doorbell rang at six. Ruby answered the door to a freshly cleaned-up Cutty. He wore the shirt Jada had given him earlier, with some black shorts. He gave Ruby a gentle hug.

"Welcome back, Cutty. How was your first day? You must be tired."

"Oh, a little for sure, but I'll survive. How about you?"

"As long as I stay out of the heat, I do okay. I mainly hang out in the basement, sewing and finishing odd projects," Ruby explained.

"I see," Cutty acknowledged. "It's nice of you to invite me for supper again."

"It's our pleasure... no bother at all," Ruby reassured him.

Just then, Jada came down the stairs in white nylon capris and a pink cold-shoulder T-shirt. She'd left her hair down but pinned the sides up.

"Hey. Nice shirt," Jada complimented Cutty.

"That's a nice color on you," Ruby added. "Is that the one from Lululemon?"

"Yes," Cutty replied. "It fits perfectly."

"That's good. I'll just go check on the hamburgers." Ruby headed toward the patio doors, located behind the kitchen.

Jada and Cutty couldn't help smiling at each other.

"I got you a little something too." Cutty placed a small bag in Jada's hand. She opened it to find a pretty bracelet featuring some pink and white beads with a couple of rhinestone spacers.

"It's lovely!" Jada exclaimed as she slipped it onto her wrist. It was made of stretchy string and fit quite nicely. "It goes perfectly with my outfit."

"That it does," Cutty noted. "It's called a mala bracelet. The mala beads are used as a tool to help the mind focus during meditation. I bought one for myself." Cutty held up his wrist and showed Jada a similar bracelet with black and gray beads. "This one is a lava bead." Cutty pointed to a porous black stone surrounded by opaque gray beads. "You can add a drop or two of essential oils to the lava bead."

"Oh, how cool is that!" Jada exclaimed. "So you can dab on some peppermint oil if you feel a headache coming on?"

"Precisely," Cutty answered.

"Well done, Cutty. Thanks for thinking of me."

"My pleasure. I found the bracelets in a little bakery café my parents took me to called Stella Sweets. Other local artists were featured there besides the spiritual yoga jewelry," Cutty explained. "The pink-and-white one reminded me of you."

"Aw." Jada melted a little inside.

She led Cutty into the kitchen and poured them all some water. Next, she placed a plate of lettuce, sliced tomatoes, and cheese as well as some condiments on the table. Finally, she placed some hamburger buns in a basket and asked Cutty to take a seat at the table. Before too long, Ruby was back inside with a plate of well-done burgers. After washing her hands, she took her seat and led them in a prayer.

"Will Brodie be joining us tonight?" Cutty asked as he built his hamburger.

"No," Ruby replied. "He's dining at the Smiths' tonight. They're having hamburgers as well," she added, chuckling.

"That makes sense," Cutty stated. "He probably missed Chloe."

At this news, Jada's eyes almost popped out of her head. "Sorry, have I missed something?"

Cutty, in turn, looked at Ruby.

Aunt Ruby calmly finished chewing her bite of food then took a sip of water.

"Aunt Ruby?" Jada persisted.

"Brodie and Chloe are seeing each other," Ruby announced matter-of-factly.

"Since when?" Jada was dumbfounded.

"Since early July, I believe," Ruby answered.

"I see." Jada calmed herself, but she felt a little foolish. *How did I not know that my cousin has been dating my best friend?*

"These hamburgers are delicious." Cutty changed the subject, seeming to sense that Jada was ill at ease. "Did you make the beef patties from scratch?" he asked Ruby.

"Yes. It's a fairly simple recipe. You just add Lipton Onion Soup Mix to the ground beef." Ruby asked Cutty about his visit with his parents and a little about the town of Sneads Ferry.

Cutty seemed happy to discuss his visit to North Carolina. Jada and Ruby spent the remainder of their dinner listening to Cutty's stories. They shared more about Orlando and Disney World with him. One of the highlights of their trip was dining at P.F. Chang's for the first time.

"It's nice to go away once in a while and equally as nice to return home," Ruby summed up. "If you two don't mind, I need to head down to the church for a meeting about the upcoming bake sale."

"Thank you, once again, for a delightful meal, Ruby," Cutty stated. "It was a great start to my busy week."

"You're welcome. And keep your weekend free, as I plan on barbecuing this Friday or Saturday evening.

I just need to see when the reverend is free," Ruby informed him.

"I'll most definitely be available for another one of your barbecues," Cutty exclaimed.

"All right. I'll be on my way soon." Ruby placed her dishes in the sink and headed upstairs to freshen up.

Jada stood and cleared her and Cutty's plates and cutlery.

"I don't mind helping you with the dishes." Cutty followed Jada to the sink with their glasses in hand. He almost dropped one of them. "Oops, close one. Glasses are not my forte."

"I'll take all the help I can get," Jada teased. She switched the radio station from easy listening, which Ruby had chosen earlier, to a pop station with more current music. It didn't take long to put the food away.

"Bye!" Ruby called from the front entrance.

"See you," Jada replied.

"Good night, Ruby," Cutty added.

Jada began scrubbing the utensils in the sink. She rinsed them one by one and set them on the dish rack.

"You were a little surprised to learn about Brodie and Chloe?" Cutty eased into the subject.

"Yeah," Jada answered honestly. "Now that I think about it, there were subtle signs last month. But neither one of them told me they were seeing each other." Jada shrugged.

"Maybe they were worried about your reaction, since you're so close to both of them," Cutty offered.

"I can see that." Jada nodded. "But how did Aunt Ruby know?"

Cutty didn't answer. He picked up a dish towel hanging on the stove and dried the utensils.

"Oh well, as long as they're happy," Jada said thoughtfully. She put away some of the utensils that Cutty had dried. As she crossed the kitchen floor, the new song "It'll Be Fine," by Jules Montgomery, began playing on the radio. She leaned over the counter and turned up the volume. Jada liked the electronic dance song, having first heard it in Florida. She began swaying to the music. Cutty turned and noticed her dancing as words poured from the radio:

"It'll be fine (she said)
Hittin' up clubs and spending all our money
Showin' off to all our friends and drinkin' Henny
We've been shakin' and swayin'
Dancing on top of speakers
Doing what we gotta do."

Cutty was mesmerized as Jada grooved to the beat.

"Don't stop, it feels so right you got my number
We've been hanging out all summer
Yeah, ain't no rest for the wicked
Oh, don't stop, don't stop, don't stop."

Jada moved toward Cutty. He began to dance with her, the dish towel draped over his left shoulder. It was invigorating for both of them, as they were caught up in the moment. The first line repeated again.

"It'll be fine (she said)."

Before long, Jada took Cutty's hands and held them up, all the while swaying her hips to the chorus. She turned her back to him, and they danced in time with each other while Cutty's arms encircled Jada. They swayed back and forth. Then she turned again, facing Cutty once more and releasing his hands. They continued enjoying the song, raising their hands in the air, hips gyrating, dancing until the end of the song.

"Wow. Some dance moves!" Cutty exclaimed.

"Why, thank you." Jada walked over to the radio and turned the volume down. "You're a pretty good dancer yourself."

They grinned at one another.

"Are you ready for some ice cream?" Jada asked.

"Sure thing." Cutty wiped a little sweat off his brow with the back of his hand.

After preparing two bowls of Ben & Jerry's pistachio ice cream, Jada suggested they sit in the living room. Cutty followed her to the large sofa.

"I guess you could say we earned our dessert tonight, after that epic dancing," Cutty announced.

"We sure did." Jada giggled.

"I wonder if Brodie got ice cream."

"I'm sure the Smiths are feeding him well. They're amazing cooks. I've enjoyed many great meals there over the years," Jada reminisced.

"You and Chloe will have to maintain your friendship now that she and Brodie are dating."

Lori Lupul

"Along with everything else changing. Going to college, her starting nursing school, and now to find out she's dating Brodie. She'll have no time for me," Jada surmised.

Cutty placed his empty bowl on the coffee table in front of them. Jada followed suit, though she hadn't quite finished her ice cream. She turned and faced Cutty while bending her knees and folding her legs underneath herself. She gently took his wrist and stroked it lightly with her free hand, gazing down at their palms while doing so.

Cutty took a deep breath. "You know, Jada, you'll soon be busy with cheerleading practice, studying, and..." Cutty paused.

"And what?" Jada probed. She wasn't sure about where the conversation was headed.

"Well," Cutty continued, "there'll be many opportunities for you, not to mention many new people you'll cross paths with."

Jada searched Cutty's eyes for his intent. "Do you mean boys?" she asked, rather surprised.

"That's precisely what I mean." Cutty seemed relieved Jada understood him.

Jada was bewildered. "How can you say that?"

"Well, I just... I thought I'd mention it because I don't want to hold you back."

"Hold me back from what? Boys?" Jada queried.

"Yes, boys. There'll be many fine ones on the basketball team, for starters."

88

"Not interested," Jada replied stubbornly.

"Don't shy away from meeting new people," Cutty offered. "Besides, Jada, I'm twenty-four years old."

"Age isn't about a number, Cutty. It's a state of mind," Jada said.

"I just want the best for you, Jada, and for you to be open to new prospects—"

"Oh, for goodness' sake, Cutty." Jada placed her arms around Cutty's neck, rolling her eyes. "Don't you get it? You fill my soul with joy." She pressed her cheek to his, giving him a gentle squeeze.

"That's nice," Cutty uttered. "Don't put me on too high a pedestal."

"You have so many fine attributes, Cutty Jones," Jada continued. "You are hardworking, handsome, fit, a gentleman, and you show empathy toward others."

"That is most kind of you." Cutty sounded touched by her words.

Jada released her hold on Cutty but not before gently kissing the side of his head. She looked into his eyes. "It's all true, every word. And I am not interested in meeting any boys, not now, not ever." Jada leaned her head on Cutty's chest and draped her free arm across his stomach.

"All right, shawty." Cutty gently stroked Jada's back with his left arm.

"Well, I'm sure glad that we got that pink elephant out of the room."

Cutty chuckled. "How do you know it's not a blue elephant?"

Jada giggled, which made Cutty chuckle more. "Or maybe it's just elephant, no color," he added.

Before long, Jada confessed, "You had me worried for a second."

"What about?"

"I mean, you know where I stand, but…"

"Listen, Jada. I stand right beside you," Cutty proclaimed softly.

At that, Jada's face lit up. "Do you really mean that?"

"Absolutely. Look I'll show you something." Cutty extracted his iPhone from his pocket while Jada straightened. "See my screen saver?" Cutty pointed to his phone.

It revealed a picture of Jada standing beside Mickey Mouse. It was a rather nice picture of Jada, but she didn't remember seeing it before.

"Where did you get that?" Jada asked.

"Brodie sent it to me," Cutty replied.

"Brodie did? For real?" Jada was pleasantly surprised at her cousin's choice of picture.

"Mm-hmm. He sent that to me while you were all in Florida. We kind of kept tabs on one another. Texted about the gym and baseball mostly," Cutty said.

He and Brodie were both avid Baltimore Orioles fans.

"Wow." Jada was impressed.

Cutty initiated the kiss, gently cupping the back of her head and drawing her close to him. It was slow, exploratory, his tongue parting her lips, searching the depths of her mouth, each enjoying the faint taste of pistachio ice cream.

Afterward, she lay her head back onto Cutty's chest, and the two cuddled more. They didn't talk, just let things be. Cutty stroked Jada's back, which made her feel sleepy.

After a while, Cutty mentioned that he should be going home, as he had paperwork to complete at the gym. They both stood and slowly made their way to the front door. "Get some rest." Cutty noticed she looked a little fatigued. He wrapped his arms around Jada and kissed her head. "I'll see you at the gym on Wednesday?"

"Absolutely." Jada smiled sleepily.

"Perfect. Thanks again for supper." Cutty turned and let himself out the front door.

"Welcome. Good night," Jada said softly as she closed and locked the door behind him.

Chapter Eight

ON WEDNESDAY, AUGUST 13, JADA realized she had three weeks before starting college—time to get her butt in gear. In addition to buying books, she had to pick up her uniform for the cheerleading squad and purchase some tennis shoes and ankle socks to wear with it.

The anticipation of seeing Cutty mounted as she dressed in a lime-green halter top and black shorts, putting her hair in a high ponytail. She would have run to the gym, except for the risk of sweating. Opening the door, her eyes sought out her man. Not only did she find Cutty, but she saw an attractive woman talking with him. It looked like she was handing him a casserole dish. *Oh boy, is this what I have to compete with?*

To avoid any awkwardness, Jada headed straight for the cardio equipment and began her warm-up stretches. Out of the corner of her eye, she saw Cutty smiling as he headed to his suite, probably to put the food away. The woman made her way out of the gym but not before saying goodbye to one of the younger boys, most likely her son.

After returning from his suite, Cutty spoke with a couple boys who were using the punching bags. He checked their hand and wrist wrappings.

Jada finished her stretches and mounted a stationary bicycle. By the time she selected her program, she noticed Cutty heading toward her.

"Good morning, shawty. I didn't see you walk in." He grinned, seeming genuinely happy to see her.

"Hey. How's your week going?" Jada was reassured by his enthusiasm.

"Pretty good. Things are picking up. A few more boys are returning to the gym, so that's keeping me on my toes."

"Oh, good. Were you able to get through your paperwork the other night?" Jada inquired, trying to keep up her target heart rate as she pedaled.

"Yeah," he answered. "I'm making a proposal to my supervisor to set up a tutoring service for the boys once school starts. Some kids struggle with certain subjects, and I wouldn't mind helping them out, pro bono. See if I can make a difference in their academics along with their fitness and well-being. It all kind of ties together—feeling good about oneself, succeeding in school, and so on."

"What a great idea!" Jada was truly impressed. Cutty never ceased to amaze her. "When did you come up with this?"

"On my holiday," Cutty replied. "I'm hoping to see the reverend at your aunt's barbecue so I can fill him in on my idea and see how things are going with Devon's family." Cutty looked thoughtful. "It was Devon's murder that got me thinking about helping the community more. Like what could I do to help keep these kids off the streets and away from the drug scene. Anything to prevent more unnecessary deaths."

"I'm sure the reverend will be happy to hear your idea. Oh, and Aunt Ruby asked me to tell you that Saturday night works best for the barbecue. That's when Rev Joe can make it."

"Perfect. Lookin' forward to it." Cutty seemed pleased. "How have you been feeling?" he asked gently.

"Oh, I'm fine," Jada replied, caught a little off guard by his question. "You mean about the other night?"

"Yeah. I don't mean to pry. You just seemed a little tired is all."

"Yeah, I was," Jada agreed. She felt slightly flushed, as it was hard to talk while doing cardio.

Cutty placed a hand on her forearm. "I'm glad we had a chance to talk." Cutty smiled knowingly.

"Me too." Jada returned Cutty's smile.

"I'll let you focus on your cardio."

"Okay," Jada responded happily as Cutty turned and walked away.

A Sweetpea in Baltimore

The doorbell rang at ten sharp on Thursday morning. Jada opened the door and greeted Chloe with a big hug. "Nice to see you, girlfriend!" Jada exclaimed.

"You too. How was your trip?" Chloe asked.

"It was awesome! We'd go back to Florida again. Amazing shopping there and tons of restaurants." Jada locked the front door and sat on the top step to tie her running shoes. She handed Chloe a small bag with the Disney World logo on it.

"What's this?" Chloe asked.

"It's just something little."

Chloe opened the bag to find some Mickey Mouse crystal icon fashion earrings in a silver setting. "Aw, they're lovely. Thank you."

"Welcome," Jada responded. "There was so much to choose from, so I just kept it simple."

"Well, you know I love bling," Chloe commented.

They started walking toward the church, taking their usual route.

"How've you been?" Jada asked.

"Good, especially since you and Brodie are back from your trip." Chloe smiled. "I have something to tell you."

"About you and Brodie?"

"Yeah, how did you know? When did you figure it out?"

"Auntie told me on Monday night. Cutty was there too. Seems like everybody knew but me."

"Yeah, sorry. He saw Brodie and me together at the gym a few times last month."

"When did this all happen?" Jada inquired.

"I guess at prom… early June. We realized there were sparks between us. Brodie made the most adorable promposal for me back in May. It was the sweetest poem. Everything rhymed. I'll have to show it to you sometime." Chloe beamed.

"Aw, Chloe, I had no idea. You never said anything. I assumed the two of you were each other's date for prom since you've known one another so long. And you're both single."

"Yeah, my bad for holding out on you, my friend. But I didn't really know what to expect at first. Once school ended and Brodie began his new job, he invited me to come to the gym in the late afternoons so we could see one another. Then he started hanging out at my house more. It just kind of blossomed in early July, and here we are, almost mid-August."

"Well, I'm happy for you both," Jada offered. "As long as he treats you like a queen."

"Oh, that he does," Chloe replied. "He's a real gentleman. Not to mention my parents and brother adore him."

"That's good. You and I could be family someday," Jada marveled.

"How's Cutty?" Chloe asked. "You must have missed him."

"Oh, I missed him all right. You'll get to see him on Saturday at the barbecue."

"Awesome."

They passed the church and were making their usual loop.

"Are you and Cutty an item?"

"We definitely have feelings for one another," Jada proclaimed. "Cutty feels he's a little too old for me and that I'll be meeting guys at college. But I set him straight on that. Anyway, if we have a relationship, it'll happen on Cutty's time. I've pretty much done what I can without appearing too desperate."

"I see," Chloe acknowledged. "Well, you know best. But I'm here for you if ever you need to talk."

"I know that. I appreciate you," Jada replied sincerely. "Please don't say anything to Brodie. I wouldn't want any of this getting back to Cutty. The last thing I need is him thinking that I'm behaving like a crazed schoolgirl."

"Understood," Chloe agreed.

The supper on Saturday evening at the Parkers' was a hit. Everyone enjoyed the barbecue pork back ribs, baked beans, and corn bread Ruby prepared.

Partway through the dinner, Ruby asked, "Have you been eating well since you've been back from North Carolina, Cutty?"

"Very well," Cutty replied.

"I'll say. Cutty is the king of casseroles," Brodie remarked, to which he and Chloe both chuckled.

"How's that?" Ruby probed.

"Well, some of the moms of the boys at the gym like to make Cutty a casserole or two." Brodie winked at Cutty. "Especially the pretty, single ones."

Jada shot Chloe a concerned look. *This is exactly why I don't want to share anything with my cousin.* Chloe gave Jada a slight nod of understanding.

"How nice," Ruby commented.

"Sounds like a good deal to me," the reverend noted. "It's an act of kindness anytime someone shows their appreciation. As a bachelor myself, I've had my fair share of complimentary meals over the span of my career."

"Most def," Brodie said teasingly to Cutty.

Cutty took it all in stride. He didn't offer any comment on the subject of casseroles.

Well played, thought Jada.

After supper, Ruby, Jada, Brodie, and Chloe cleared the dishes and put away the food. That gave Cutty a chance to share his tutoring proposal with Rev Joe.

"I heard on the news recently that nine out of ten boys aren't reading at their grade level. It's a shame. Education is the way forward," the reverend stated emphatically. "A way to get jobs and lower poverty."

"Almost no students are proficient in math," Cutty added. "The education system needs all the help it can get."

When Cutty told him about the motivation for his idea, the reverend responded, "You know, Detective

Walker paid me a visit the other day. He's recanvassing the area. The police are not letting Devon's case go cold."

"The detective visited the gym also," Cutty responded. "I make sure the Wanted poster stays at the center of the bulletin board so the boys see it and keep it on their minds, in case they hear or remember something."

"I keep praying the police will receive an important lead, something to break the case," Rev Joe shared.

"That would be a miracle," Cutty agreed.

Ruby served up a peach crisp with Cool Whip for dessert. She gave the reverend some tea.

"Oh my, Ruby. The way you feed us, I'll have to start attending the gym with these young ones," Rev Joe exclaimed.

"Actually, Jada made the peach crisp," Ruby stated.

"It's delicious," Chloe praised.

Cutty smiled at Jada. He put his right pointer finger against his thumb and gave her the hand symbol for perfection. *She lifts and cooks.*

After dessert, Brodie and Chloe bade their farewells, and they headed off to the Smith home to hang out with Michael.

The reverend also stood and made his leave. He had to tweak his sermon for Sunday morning. He was very gracious in thanking his hostess, and Ruby was humble in return. She thrived on feeding her family and friends.

"I'll just head down to the basement for a bit. I need to fix something I've been working on," Ruby informed Jada and Cutty.

"Well, if I don't see you later, thanks for dinner. It was nice catching up with everyone," Cutty added.

"You are most welcome. I'm glad to hear you're not going hungry at the gym," Ruby replied.

"Would you like to sit outside on our back deck, Cutty?" Jada was quick to change the subject.

"That sounds lovely." Cutty followed Jada through the screened patio doors and stepped onto a comfortable deck with a roof.

The barbecue stood off to one side, while a double-bench swing took up most of the other side of the deck, accompanied by two cushioned wicker chairs. What caught Cutty's eye was the small yet dense garden at the back of the fenced-in yard.

"You guys have a garden?" he asked.

"Yeah. Nothing too extravagant," Jada replied.

"Can I see it?" Cutty asked.

"Of course." Jada led him down the steps off the porch and onto a small redbrick pathway. They passed rows of potatoes, carrots, green onions, lettuce, and radishes. The garden was well tended and ready for harvest in some areas.

"What is that heavenly smell?" Cutty breathed in a delicate, intoxicating scent.

"That would be the sweet peas." Jada pointed to the multicolored blossoms hanging from the vines across the entire back fence with the exception of the small gate.

Cutty was enthralled by the sight. So many hues to take in—white, coral, and a few of shades of pink and purple. "Sweet peas, you say? I've never seen them before."

"Yes. The Latin name is *Lathyrus odoratus*, which translates to 'pea' and 'fragrant.' They originated in Cyprus, Sicily, and Southern Italy."

"Amazing," Cutty exclaimed.

"My uncle Roy planted the original garden. He loved sweet peas," Jada explained. "We've kept it up as best we can ever since Uncle Roy passed away."

"Must be a fair bit of work."

"We all plant the vegetables together. Then the garden just requires watering and weeding. Since Brodie started his new job this summer, mostly my aunt and I have been sharing the upkeep. Our neighbor looked after it while we were away."

"How do you get the sweet peas to grow upward like that?"

"It's all in the mesh backing. The sweet peas grow as a climbing vine, so once their tendrils attach to the bottom of the mesh, they just keep growing upward until they bloom," Jada enlightened him. "The key to growing sweet peas successfully is all in the germination of the seeds in the fall. We plant the seeds in small six-pack containers and keep them in the house over winter. Then, in midspring, we plant the seeds in the garden once the soil can be worked."

"Interesting," Cutty said. "And you learned this from your uncle Roy?"

"Yeah, Aunt Ruby taught Brodie and me a little about gardening also. It's therapeutic. Plus, we enjoy eating the vegetables at the end of the summer."

"Maybe you could teach me sometime," Cutty suggested. "I never had a garden growing up. My mom likes to have a few flowerpots in the summer. But nothing quite as lovely as these sweet peas." Cutty stared at the flowers.

"For sure," Jada replied happily. "Would you like to sit on the bench swing?"

"Okay."

Cutty followed Jada back up the steps, and they sat together on the porch swing. Wearing a sundress with a green floral print on it, Jada had left her hair hanging down. She shifted the bulk of her tresses to the side opposite Cutty as they sat down. As she gazed upward, she caught Cutty staring at her, smiling.

"You look beautiful tonight," he said earnestly.

"Thanks," Jada replied softly.

Cutty placed his hand gently on her neck as he leaned in for a kiss. His soft, warm lips stimulated Jada in ways she wasn't accustomed to. When they finally broke apart, she slowly opened her eyes.

"You smell lovely too," Cutty complimented.

"Aw, I could listen to you all night." Jada smiled up at Cutty in return. She was wearing Fantasy by Britney

Spears, another one of her purchases from Orlando. She was pleased Cutty liked it.

Cutty kissed her again, that one lasting longer than the first. Jada didn't want it to end.

When it finally did, Cutty softly caressed Jada's shoulder. "You smell as lovely as those sweet peas," he proclaimed.

"I'll take that as a compliment." Jada liked his line of thought. She lay her head on his shoulder, and they chatted for a while. Both were acutely aware of the evening sounds. People laughing in the distance, a lawnmower whirring a few houses away, an airplane flying overhead.

The pair discussed their plans for the following day, Sunday. Cutty informed Jada that he was attending a car show at the Baltimore Convention Center with Elias and Levi. They would probably grab a bite to eat afterward, while they were out.

"Sounds fun," Jada exclaimed. "Chloe and I are going shopping tomorrow for school stuff. I need tennis shoes for my cheerleading uniform."

"When does practice begin?"

"We have one the first week of school. After that, it'll be three practices per week for two hours at a time," Jada replied.

"Plus performances at the basketball games starting in November. Busy schedule," Cutty noted.

"For sure," Jada agreed. "But at least I have good study habits. I plan on doing my coursework between classes as often as I can."

"You'll ace it, I'm sure," Cutty said. "You'll just have to plan some down time so you don't burn out."

"Yeah… I'll keep that in mind." Jada squeezed his arm lightly.

Cutty looked at Jada thoughtfully. He had no doubt she would be able to balance her life. She appeared to have a good head on her shoulders. "I should be on my way home."

"May I walk you partway, at least?" Jada enticed.

"You may." Cutty rose and offered Jada a hand up.

They walked through the town house, and that time, Jada chose some comfy flip-flops to wear. She locked the front door on her way out. When she descended the steps, Cutty was waiting for her with an outstretched hand. Jada clasped it readily, and they walked contentedly, holding hands. It gave her such pleasure that he openly displayed his affection toward her.

When they reached the end of the block, they stood in front of an electronics store, which was closed for the evening. The windows were covered with metal bars for security.

"This is where we part, Sweet Pea." Cutty leaned down and planted a soft kiss on the side of Jada's face. "I'll see you at the gym on Monday?"

"Of course." Jada liked Cutty's new endearment for her.

The pair unclasped their hands. Both were grinning as they turned and walked to their respective homes.

Chapter Nine

CUTTY MANAGED TO GET A run in before opening the boxing gym Monday morning. It had been a busy weekend for him, spending time with Jada and her family Saturday evening then hanging out with his friends most of Sunday. It felt good to be back in his routine. Although he missed his parents, he made a point of calling them every week. He hoped to see them again at Thanksgiving.

The equipment looked a little dusty, so Cutty filled a pail with soapy water and began wiping the punching bags with a rag. At the sound of the door opening, he looked up to see Tyrell and D'andre walk in.

"Hey, guys," Cutty exclaimed.

"My man, how's it going?" Tyrell asked.

The boys took turns clasping hands with Cutty.

"It's going well. Are you guys working out this morning or sparring?"

"We're gonna work out. And spot for one another," D'andre replied.

"Sounds good. Let me know if you need anything," Cutty offered.

"How about cranking up the tunes a little?" Tyrell asked.

The boys liked their hip-hop music.

"All right." Cutty made his way to the stereo and turned up the volume slightly. He didn't mind obliging the boys once in a while. They were, after all, good kids. And Cutty enjoyed their company. Truth be told, Cutty was fond of all the kids who utilized the boxing gym. He had developed good relationships with most of them and was even getting to know some of their families. That was why having his tutoring proposal accepted was so important. He felt his services would give him a sense of purpose, an adjunct to supervising the gym and working part-time as a massage therapist. He took another look at his file folder to proofread it one more time. He planned on seeing his supervisor later in the day.

Before long, Jada walked in dressed in a green-and-black camouflage tank top and black shorts. Cutty glanced up briefly then did a double take once he realized who it was.

"Mm-hmm," Cutty said under his breath. He liked her outfit that morning. It made her look like she was in charge and ready for action.

"Hey, Cutty." Jada smiled at him. "How's your day shaping up?"

"It's going well," Cutty replied. "But it's gonna be even better now that you're here."

"Aw, you're too sweet." Jada walked right up to Cutty and gave him a hug.

"I was thinking about making a beef stew. I got a recipe from my mom. It has all kinds of vegetables in it."

"Sounds delicious," Jada commented.

"Oh, it is," Cutty confirmed. "I was wondering if you'd join me for supper tomorrow, say around six."

"I'd love to. Can I at least bring something?" Jada asked.

"No thanks. I've got it covered."

"Are you sure?"

"Yeah, just come over. We can spend some time together, maybe watch a little TV."

"Sounds good. How was the car show yesterday?"

"It was great. Elias was in his element, checking out the new BMW line." Cutty chuckled. "But it's not like I'll be buying a BMW in my lifetime." Cutty didn't own a car. He used public transportation when necessary. And he was quite frugal with his money. Although it wasn't lucrative by any means, he managed to live quite comfortably off his salary from the gym, while saving all of the income from his part-time massage therapy job. The only payment he had was his student loan debt, which wasn't huge. He'd always worked part-time while attending college, and his parents had helped him out a little, for which Cutty was very grateful.

"Did the three of you go out for supper?" Jada asked.

"Yeah, we dined at the Blue Agave restaurant over on Light Street... Mexican cuisine. How about you and Chloe? Did you two get your shopping done?"

"Oh yeah. We got some retail therapy." Jada rolled her eyes.

"Good. But I hope you left some merchandise for the other students," Cutty teased.

"Don't worry. We did," Jada said. "I should probably start my workout now." A few more boys had entered the gym. They would be needing Cutty's assistance shortly.

Cutty looked to see who they were. "All right, talk to you later." He made his way over to the boys.

Jada arrived at the boxing gym shortly before six the next evening wearing a denim miniskirt and a pink-and-orange-patterned short-sleeved blouse. She found Cutty putting away some equipment as the last few boys headed out the door.

"Hey." Cutty nodded at Jada and smiled. "Good timing. Things are just wrapping up here."

"Perfect. Can I help you with anything?" Jada offered.

"Nah, thanks though." Cutty walked over to the front door and locked it.

Jada took a moment to read the bulletin board. Nothing had changed. Cutty kept it well organized. "How did it go with your supervisor yesterday?"

"It went well." Cutty sounded confident. "She's gonna show my proposal to her boss then give me the green light once it's approved."

"Aw. I'm sure they'll love your idea. If only there were more selfless people like you to advocate for change. It's the kids who will benefit, which will improve our community. A ripple effect," Jada stated.

"I hope so." Cutty shut off the lights, and the two made their way toward the door to Cutty's suite.

Once inside, Jada was met with the delicious aroma of stew. She did a quick survey of Cutty's bachelor apartment. It wasn't overly big, yet it seemed to have everything a single person could need. The kitchen, on the left side of the suite, had a refrigerator, stove, microwave, and even a dishwasher. A small rectangular table with four chairs separated the sofa, lounge chair, and television area from the kitchen. A door also stood on the back wall, near the kitchen table, which Jada assumed led to the back alley. A queen-size bed along with two night tables stood at the other end of the suite. A closet and washroom were located near the bed to the right of the boxing gym entrance.

"Nice crib you have here," Jada complimented.

"Thanks. Nothing fancy, but it'll do." Cutty turned on the television. "I'm just going to change my clothes," he announced, handing Jada the remote.

"No worries." Jada took a seat on the couch as Cutty headed toward the washroom. She put on a local Baltimore news channel.

When the news program switched to the sports updates, Jada looked at her phone. She spent some time browsing Instagram, where she saw a picture of Brodie and Chloe together. *Wow, these two are out in the open now.* She couldn't help but notice how happy they looked.

Cutty emerged from the washroom a few minutes later, looking sharp in khaki shorts and a black golf shirt. "How about we have us some stew?" he suggested, clapping his hands. He walked over to the oven, donned some oven mitts, and opened the door. Carefully lifting out a large enamel roasting dish, he placed it on top of the stove. Next, he lifted the lid and checked the meat. "Looks ready."

"It smells so good." Jada stood and made her way to the kitchen.

"It's self-serve," Cutty announced. He handed Jada a large ladle and a dinner plate. She eagerly served herself two scoops of the stew and headed for the table. Cutty got two glasses of water and placed them along with some buns and butter on top of the kitchen table. He served himself some stew and joined Jada.

After taking her first couple of bites, Jada exclaimed, "This is probably the best stew I've ever tasted! And you know my aunt Ruby is an amazing cook." In addition to beef, the stew contained potatoes, carrots, turnips, celery, and onions.

"Yeah. My mom is a pretty good cook also. She enjoys trying out new recipes in her retirement."

"Aw. What type of work did your parents do?"

"My dad was a firefighter. He spent over forty-five years of his life working for the Baltimore City Fire Department. He was the captain of his unit for the last several years of his career before he retired."

"Really? That's amazing." Jada was impressed.

"And my mom was a neonatal nurse at Saint Agnes Hospital. She loved caring for all the babies, especially the sick ones. I think it gave her a deep sense of purpose, especially since she couldn't have children of her own." Cutty paused briefly. "She worked full-time up until her late thirties. Then, once they became foster parents, she worked part-time so she could be there for all of us," Cutty explained.

"It sounds like your parents are wonderful people," Jada acknowledged.

"They sure are," Cutty stated. "I was pretty lucky to be placed in their care. They say there's a reason for everything. You know, I'm not proud of the choices I made back in middle school, but I sure ended up in a loving home with great parents. It was the silver lining to the cloud," Cutty reminisced.

"Well, I think you turned out to be a pretty decent guy," Jada praised. "And a great cook."

Jada's last comment made Cutty smile. The pair finished their supper in silence, savoring the last few mouthfuls.

"Help yourself to some more stew, if you like," Cutty offered.

"Actually, I'm full. Thanks though," Jada replied. "It's my turn to help with the dishes." They both stood and cleared the table. Jada rinsed the dishes and placed them in the dishwasher while Cutty put the stew into a plastic food container. Then he placed the roasting dish in the sink with hot, soapy water.

"Shall we sit on the couch for a bit and watch TV?" Cutty asked.

"Sounds good. You've had a busy day," Jada noted as they walked toward the sofa. "Are those your parents?" Jada pointed to an eight-by-ten framed photo of Cutty in his convocation robe and cap, surrounded by a middle-aged couple.

"Yeah. Marvin and Delores," Cutty answered fondly, taking a seat on the couch.

"A nice-looking bunch," Jada complimented.

As Jada sat down beside Cutty, she felt a slight pain between her upper shoulder blades. She wrapped her left arm up and over her right shoulder and gave it a little massage.

"Everything okay?" Cutty asked.

"I've been experiencing some tenderness in my upper back lately. Probably from weight lifting," Jada shared.

"I can take a look," Cutty suggested. He stood. "Just lie on the couch facedown."

Jada did as Cutty asked, albeit carefully since she was wearing a mini skirt and didn't want to have a wardrobe malfunction.

Cutty kneeled beside her. Fortunately, Jada's top only covered her upper back slightly, while flaring out to the sides, exposing her lower back like an inverted V shape. Cutty began to gently massage the right side of her upper back.

"Ohhh," Jada exhaled. She'd never had a massage before.

"Tell me if anything hurts," Cutty told her. He massaged Jada's right side and checked her left upper back, maneuvering around her bra strap. He spent several minutes manipulating the knots there.

Once Jada got over the initial tenderness, she began to relax and feel the tension in her back release. Although her position was compromised, she felt quite comfortable in Cutty's hands. She envisioned his flexed biceps as he manipulated her soft tissue. His buff physique had piqued her interest from day one. It was all she could do to focus on her breathing while he completed his task.

"You've probably been overdoing it. I'll take a look at your routine next time you work out. Have you been drinking enough water?" Cutty asked.

"I try, though sometimes I don't get eight cups down."

"You can sit up now." Cutty stood to make room for Jada to sit up on the couch. He walked into the kitchen and filled a glass with cold water from the tap.

When Cutty returned to the couch, he offered a composed Jada the glass. "Drink up," he gently ordered. "Massage therapy stimulates the circulation to the muscles, which brings nutrients to the area more quickly. And it also stimulates the lymphatic system, which helps remove the toxins. Drinking water helps the body flush out those toxins."

"I see," Jada replied. It wasn't just her muscles that were stimulated.

Cutty began to search the guide on the television, using the remote.

"Thank you for your professional services," Jada spoke demurely. "I'll be sure to recommend you."

"My pleasure." Cutty smiled in response. "And send patients my way. I'd be much obliged." He chuckled. It was seven forty-five. "How does the *Big Bang Theory* sound?"

"Sounds good." Jada continued to slowly sip her water.

Cutty gently took Jada's left hand in his right one and held it, turning his attention to the TV.

Jada tried to focus on the show but couldn't help but sneak glances at her host from time to time. *I wish he'd just kiss me already.*

It wasn't until the second commercial break that Cutty made his move. "It's a rerun," he said, releasing her hand. He turned his body slightly toward Jada and leaned in.

Ready at the helm, Jada clasped the back of Cutty's head and met his kiss full-on.

As their tongues reconnected, Jada slid her hand down the side of Cutty's neck and onto his shoulder. It was her turn to massage, exploring his chiselled form, something she had yearned to do for some time.

Cutty placed his hand on Jada's waist. His thumb gently explored the patch of exposed skin, where her blouse raised up from the skirt. Jada inhaled and held her breath for a few seconds as his hand lifted upward and grazed her breast. She felt lost in heady delight as his fingers lifted her bra and began teasing her nipple.

"Ohhh…" Jada softly exhaled. So enraptured by his ardor, she didn't want the moment to end. As she was preparing to lean back onto the sofa, Cutty pulled away.

"I need some air." Cutty spoke softly.

Disappointed, Jada slowly collected herself. She sensed that he didn't want to take things further. Cutty encircled Jada's shoulders with his arm, and the pair watched another episode of the *Big Bang Theory*.

By nine o'clock, Cutty announced, "Well, it's probably time I walked you home." He stood and offered his hand to help Jada up. When she was standing, Cutty pulled Jada into a hug.

Jada responded by wrapping her arms around Cutty's midsection. "This was such a relaxing evening." The words felt lame.

"Mm-hmm. Just the way I like it." Cutty gently rubbed Jada's back. Then he led Jada to the back door.

They stepped out into the alley and walked, holding hands, toward the street. The traffic wasn't too busy at that time of night. A few cars passed as they walked along the sidewalk. A dark-colored SUV passed with its front windows rolled all the way down. Loud hip-hop music played on its radio, the base almost deafening.

"Ouch," Cutty exclaimed. "That's not necessary. They'll be deaf before they reach thirty." He shook his head. A Baltimore City Police cruiser drove by them, traveling the opposite direction as the SUV. "It's not likely that SUV gets pulled over," he added.

The two strolled leisurely toward Jada's home with not much conversation. Once they arrived at the Parker town house, Jada stood on the bottom step, facing Cutty.

"Thanks again for an amazing time." She beamed into his eyes.

"You're welcome. I hope your back feels better." With that said, Cutty leaned toward Jada, who was almost at his level, and kissed her.

Jada responded wholeheartedly. She could get used to this.

"I'll see you tomorrow morning at the gym?" Cutty asked as they broke apart.

"Most definitely," Jada purred. She watched as Cutty turned and walked back toward his suite. Then she climbed the remaining three steps and let herself into her home.

Chapter Ten

CUTTY CHECKED THE TIME AGAIN on Wednesday morning. It was eleven o'clock, and still no Jada. She usually arrived at the gym around ten on days she worked out. A few more minutes passed, and Cutty was about to text her, when Jada suddenly entered through the front door. She wore a pretty yellow sundress and carried a backpack.

"There you are," Cutty exclaimed. "I was just about to text you and make sure you were still coming to your workout."

"Yeah. I'm sorry, I should have let you know I would be late," Jada responded. "I had a doctor's appointment at ten."

"Everything okay?" Cutty looked concerned.

"Yeah. It was just my annual checkup." Jada smiled.

"Phew! I was a little worried." Cutty smiled back.

"I have to change. See you in a few minutes." Jada headed toward the women's washroom.

A few minutes later, she emerged wearing the pink Lululemon tank top and cropped leggings she'd worn to the gym her first time back after her holiday. Cutty was helping some boys with wrapping their hands, so Jada proceeded to the cardio area and began her warm-up exercises.

After completing her cardio on the elliptical, Jada selected some arm weights. As she was about to begin her routine, Cutty was by her side. As promised, he checked Jada's routine and was able to correct her form on her overhead triceps extension. Cutty instructed Jada to keep her elbows close to her forehead as she lowered the fifteen-pound weight behind her head then extend her arms straight up.

"Your form is actually quite good. Make sure to drink all your water and then some," Cutty reminded her, pointing to her water bottle.

"I'll try," Jada responded. "Will you be working at the chiropractic office tomorrow evening?"

"Yeah," Cutty replied. "Business is picking up."

"That's good. You're an amazing massage therapist." Jada smiled.

"Hmm, thanks." Cutty placed his hand on her forearm, giving it a gentle squeeze. His touch stirred her inner core. "Let me know how your back feels after today."

"Okay." Jada would be down for another massage in a heartbeat.

As Jada began her final stretches, Cutty asked, "Would you be up for going to a movie with me on Saturday evening, if you aren't busy?"

"I'd love to," Jada answered happily, glad she didn't have any plans that night.

"Okay, then. I'll see what's playing and give you some options." One of the boys approached Cutty. He had to get back to supervising the boxing ring. "See you Friday."

"You betcha," Jada responded cheerfully.

Friday began as a busy day at the gym. So many boys in attendance had Cutty on his toes, and they were amped. *Everyone must want to look their best for school.*

Cutty waved at Jada as she entered the gym shortly after ten. He couldn't leave the boys he was supervising, as they were sparring novices. And as far as Cutty was concerned, it was the most important training aspect of being a boxer. Sparring was where one actually learned to fight, to see what worked and what didn't while finding out what needed to be improved. He didn't agree with the sink-or-swim method, whereby trainers put new fighters in the ring only to be destroyed by a more experienced one. Just like learning the basic footwork, defense, and all of the punches, sparring was to develop skills, not to determine a winner.

He was so engrossed with his trainees that Cutty barely felt D'andre's tap on his shoulder.

"What's up?" Cutty inquired.

"Not sure, boss. Take a look." D'andre lifted his head in the direction of the cardio equipment and weights.

Cutty turned in that direction to see two young men standing near Jada, engaged in some type of conversation. "Hold on a couple of minutes there," he told the boys in the ring. He made his way over to the visitors. He didn't recognize either of them. As Cutty approached them, he could hear the taller one speaking.

"Why don't you get your phone out and take my number? I'm sure a pretty thing like you wants to have a good time later." The stranger spoke a little too confidently.

"I don't have my phone with me," Jada responded.

"Can I help you guys?" Cutty asked.

"It's all good. We can help ourselves," the tall one replied. He barely glanced at Cutty. He focused his attention back on Jada. "My buddy will get some paper from the bulletin board over there and write my number down for you. Better yet, you can give me your number, and I'll punch it into my phone." He leered at Jada.

"That won't be necessary," Cutty stated assertively. "Are you boys planning to register at this gym?"

"Nah, we don't need to make it all official," the tall one said. "My buddy and I just wanted to check it out. Maybe we'll hang out here once in a while." He wore a thick yellow-gold chain around his neck and diamond studs in both ears.

"You need to be registered in order to use this facility," Cutty said.

"Well, I'm just talking to this girl. No need to register." The tall one turned his back on Cutty and placed a hand on Jada's arm. "Ain't that right, miss?"

Cutty saw red. He was quick to grab the guy's arm off Jada. But the dude wasn't having it. He quickly drew his arm up, ready to throw a punch at Cutty. No stranger to a dirty boxing technique, the latter took a step back, baiting his aggressor, then stepped forward, smashing his head into the guy's chest. Cutty lifted his head, simultaneously lifting his opponent's, and threw a hook into the guy's chin.

"Ahhhh…" The fella groaned, cradling his chin with his hand.

"Get out now," Cutty demanded.

D'andre and Tyrell were at his side by that time.

"Yeah? What gives you the authority?" the shorter guy asked rudely.

"I manage this gym, and that makes me responsible for the well-being of everyone who sets foot in here," Cutty replied, seething.

The shorter guy scoffed.

The bejeweled one glared at Cutty and muttered, "So much for my welfare. This ain't the only gym in town. We'll find ourselves another one."

As they swaggered toward the exit, the tall guy spit on the gym floor.

Cutty was about to respond to the strangers, but intuition told him to bite his tongue. *So disrespectful.*

"Good riddance, hey, boss?" Tyrell asked once the strangers had left.

"Yeah," D'andre agreed. "We don't need that around here."

Cutty stared a moment at the door. "Thanks for having my back." He looked at both D'andre and Tyrell. "You mind watching the boys in the ring for a few minutes?"

"Sure thing," Tyrell answered.

He and D'andre walked over to the ring.

"May I have a word with you, Jada?" Cutty nodded toward his suite.

"Of course." Jada followed him to the door in silence.

Once inside, Cutty shut the door and held both of Jada's arms with his hands. "You okay, Sweet Pea?" he asked worriedly.

"Yeah, just creeped out," Jada responded. "How about you?"

"I'm pissed. I didn't see that comin'. Last thing we need around here is a bunch of punks causing a ruckus." He would have to write up an incident report about the unwanted visitors.

Jada nodded. "Don't worry about me."

Cutty wasn't convinced. "I'd feel better if you took some boxing lessons."

"The university offers some self-defence courses on Saturdays, starting in September."

"Yeah? Maybe you should enroll in them," Cutty stated.

"Good idea. I'll look online when I get home."

"You do that." Cutty gave Jada a long hug.

"Thanks for looking out for me today." Jada squeezed Cutty's upper body with her arms and buried her head in his chest.

"All right." Cutty broke away first. "We should probably head back inside now." Cutty led Jada to the door. He studied her body language as she headed into the gym, just to make sure she wasn't visibly shaken.

Cutty rang the doorbell of the Parker town house at a quarter past six on Saturday evening. Since time was tight, he had arranged for Elias to drive them to the movie theater about ten blocks away.

Jada was ready, dressed in distressed light-denim cropped pants and a cream-colored sleeveless top. She had a light navy sweater draped over her arm in case it cooled off for their walk home. She wore her hair down and had put extra curls in it for the date.

"Hey," she greeted with her beautiful smile.

He looked handsome in a light-green T-shirt and khaki shorts.

"Hey, Sweet Pea. You look lovely." Cutty bent to give Jada a quick kiss.

"Aw, thanks," Jada replied as she turned and locked the front door. The pair made their way to a BMW waiting near the sidewalk. Cutty opened the rear door for

Jada, and they slid into the back seat. Elias and Samantha greeted Jada from the front seats.

"Hi, guys! Nice car. I've never ridden in a BMW before," Jada exclaimed. She took in her surroundings after buckling her seat belt. Although it was an older model, it was well maintained.

"Thanks," Elias responded. "It was in rough shape when it first came into the shop… a repo. I've put many hours into refurbishing her. You could say she's my baby." He pulled out into the street and began driving toward the theater.

"Will you be joining us for the movie tonight?" Jada inquired.

"No, not this time," Samantha stated. "We're meeting with both our parents shortly to go over some wedding details."

"And to have some dessert," Elias added.

"Aw, congratulations!" Jada exclaimed. "Cutty mentioned that you two are getting married next summer."

"Thanks," Samantha replied. "We'll have our hands full with all the little details. The year will go by fast."

Cutty sat quietly, holding Jada's hand, admiring how easy she was with his friends. She looked so stylish and feminine in her outfit. He noted that she'd chosen comfortable sandals as well as a small cross-body purse.

Elias was playing a local R & B station on the car radio at a decent level.

As they neared the theater, Cutty noticed some empty spaces. "You can pull in here, Eli. We can walk the rest of the way."

Elias signaled and pulled the car in toward the sidewalk.

"Thanks for driving us. It's a treat," Jada said.

"Yeah, thanks, guys," Cutty chimed in.

"No worries," Elias replied. "It was on our way."

"Enjoy your movie." Samantha waved as Jada and Cutty exited the car.

Cutty had purchased the tickets in advance for the movie *Sin City: A Dame to Kill For*, so they didn't have to wait in line.

"Would you like a drink or popcorn?" he offered once inside the building.

"I'm good, still full from supper," Jada replied.

"Me too," Cutty agreed. "Let's pick out some good seats."

They made their way to the designated theater and climbed the stairs up to the top rows. Cutty chose an aisle seat and motioned for Jada to take the seat next to it.

Once settled, he turned a little and faced Jada. "How's your back feeling today?"

"It's better," Jada replied. "I took a bath with Epsom salts last night."

"Ah," Cutty responded. "You're looking quite toned these days, making gains."

"Thanks. I've enjoyed the gym. It's been a good summer so far." Jada beamed.

"It has—with the exception of yesterday." Cutty took hold of Jada's hand and gave it a little kiss. "Hopefully, you can work out during school."

"Yeah, that would be nice. I'll see what my schedule is like first, but I'm sure I can fit the gym in, even if it's only once a week. I hope I'll be seeing you more than that, though."

People were making their way into the theater, and the seats steadily filled up. Before long, the lights dimmed, and the previews began on the screen ahead of them.

Partway through the movie, Cutty had to unclasp his hand from Jada's, as it was falling asleep. Jada clasped her hand under Cutty's arm and held it for a while, giving it a little massage.

After the movie, Jada and Cutty slowly made their way out of the theater. They held hands as they walked among the throng of people. It was a lovely evening, at seventy-four degrees. It was twilight, as the sun had set just before eight o'clock, and fewer people were on the streets as they leisurely strolled toward Jada's home.

"Did you enjoy the movie?" Jada asked.

"It was all right," Cutty responded. "It's nice to get out once in a while."

"For sure," Jada agreed. "It's good to have a break from all that exercising."

They were about six blocks from their destination. Partway down the commercial block they were walking along was a vacant alley. They were so enthralled with each other that they didn't notice the two shadowy figures ahead of them.

Cutty almost bumped into the taller one, who said harshly, "Watch where you're going."

Looking upward, Cutty recognized the punks from the gym.

"Look who we have here. It's the boss man." The tall guy smirked as he fondled the thick gold chain around his neck. It looked gaudy up close.

Cutty tried slowly backing away.

"Hold on," the tall guy ordered, brandishing a medium-sized knife.

The shorter guy grabbed both of Jada's arms and forcibly held them behind her back while dragging her into the alley. Jada gasped.

"Go easy there, man," Cutty responded, trying to avert danger. He held his right hand in the air. "Let the lady go."

"You think you've got power out here on the street?" The guy with the knife scoffed. "This is our territory." He spit on the ground and waved his knife.

The attackers wore baggy jeans and sweatshirts. From the way the tall one spoke, Cutty assumed they were gangsters.

"Look, we aren't asking for trouble," Cutty stated. "Just let go of the lady, and you two can deal with me."

He bravely took a step forward, toward the knife-wielding man.

"Stop right there," the thug demanded.

He swung at Cutty with his free hand. Cutty was quick to block him, but it was too late. The guy sliced the right side of Cutty's body just above his waist. Jada screamed loudly as Cutty dropped to his knees. Blood oozed from his wound.

"Ah." Cutty winced in pain as he tried to get his bearings while keeping an eye on Jada. He had no idea what the thugs would do next.

Suddenly, the shorter guy shouted a warning to his partner. "The po-po are up."

With that, the assailants ditched their prey and ran down the back alley, jumping into a waiting vehicle.

Jada watched as the dark-colored SUV sped off then quickly ran to Cutty's side. "Oh, God! Cutty, are you okay?"

Cutty turned and sat on his butt, holding his left hand over the fresh knife wound.

Jada bundled up the sweater she had been carrying and gave it to Cutty. "Here, use this to apply pressure."

Cutty lifted his hand off the wound and placed the sweater over it, followed by his left hand.

Meanwhile, the police cruiser backed up, sounded its siren a couple of times, and flashed its lights steadily as it pulled up to the sidewalk where Jada huddled over Cutty. Once the patrol car was parked, two Baltimore City Police officers quickly exited the vehicle. They had their guns drawn as one officer raised his badge and yelled, "Police!"

The other officer was quick to order, "Stay right where you are, and show me your hands, both of you!"

Jada did as she was told, while Cutty raised his right hand partially. It was too painful for him to lift it any farther.

"Officers, my friend was stabbed. We were attacked by two guys. They ran off down the back alley just as you drove by," Jada tearfully explained. "Please, can you call an ambulance? He's bleeding."

The officer who drove the police cruiser clasped the radio at his shoulder and called for backup. "We're out on Lennington Avenue and Fourteenth Street, requesting 129 and an 11-41. We have two victims. One is down with a knife wound. Suspects have left the scene. Over." He headed to the trunk while communicating with his dispatcher and retrieved a first aid kit.

The second officer verified Jada's information and guarded the scene.

The first officer donned a pair of blue nitrile gloves. "How are you feeling?" He pulled the sweater away from Cutty's body and checked to make sure nothing was protruding from the wound, foreign or otherwise.

"I feel shaky. You couldn't have arrived at a better time, Officer. I don't know what would have happened if you hadn't—ohh!" Cutty exclaimed in pain as the officer applied a thick wad of gauze.

The second officer went to his vehicle and brought a water bottle back for Cutty. "Here, sip on the water a little. The ambulance is on its way. Paramedics will take good care of you once they arrive. I want you to sit calmly and quietly now."

"Yeah, everything is going to be okay. You both understand?" the first officer reiterated.

Jada and Cutty nodded.

"Are you okay?" Cutty searched Jada's face.

"I'm okay, Cutty. Please don't talk. Save your strength," she pleaded.

Within a couple of minutes, a second patrol car arrived. Two more police officers exited their cruiser, a male and a female. The second officer caught the newcomers up to speed.

The male and female officers identified themselves to Jada and Cutty. "Tell us about the suspects," the female officer said.

Jada was able to give them a description, not only of the two thugs but also of the SUV they'd sped away in. Two more patrol cars arrived, and within a short time, armed officers began searching the back alley and farther down the area.

The ambulance also arrived, and two attendants were quick to assess Cutty and take over for the first police officer.

A third paramedic approached Jada and assessed her for any wounds and visible shock. He was very focused as he took information from Jada about the attack on her and Cutty.

The first police officer also took down Jada's and Cutty's personal details for his report. Jada gave information to the best of her ability.

"You'll need to accompany me down to the police station to make a formal report about the incident this evening, Miss Stevens." The officer addressed Jada.

Jada nodded. "Yeah, of course. I'll do whatever is necessary." She noticed Cutty had been lifted onto a stretcher, and attendants were beginning to carefully load him into the ambulance. "Please, Officer, may I say goodbye to Cutty?"

The first officer turned and assessed the situation with the paramedics and their patient. "All right, but make it quick. Gotta get him to the hospital."

"Thanks." Jada slowly approached the stretcher. "How are you holding up, Cutty? Looks like you're in good hands now." She looked at him with care as she softly squeezed his left hand with her own.

"I'll be okay. I'm so sorry this happened." He winced a little.

An intravenous line ran from his left wrist in case he required a blood transfusion at the hospital. The paramedics had started Cutty on a saline solution to prevent dehydration.

"I'll come see you as soon as the police are finished taking my statement," Jada reassured him. It was time to let go of his hand. Jada backed away and watched help-lessly. "What hospital are you taking him to?" she asked the paramedic who had previously questioned her.

"Saint Agnes," he replied.

"Thanks." Jada nodded. The same one where Cutty's mom used to work. She turned back to the first officer. "I'm ready to go."

The officer escorted Jada to the back of his patrol car and assisted her with the seat belt.

"Just remain in the car. I'll let my partner know we're heading down to the station," he noted.

"Is it okay for me to text my family?" Jada inquired.

"Yes, but keep it brief, and don't give out too many details," the officer replied.

Jada group texted her aunt and Brodie. She suggested they let Cutty's friends know so they could get in touch with Cutty's family. They were both quick to respond with nothing but care and concern. Brodie asked which precinct Jada would be taken to so he could meet her to escort her home. Jada replied that she would ask the officer once he returned to the car and let them know.

Within minutes after the ambulance left, the first officer returned to the car to drive Jada to the station. "Once we get to the station, there'll be some mug shots to go through, see if you can identify your attackers. And you'll need to provide a written statement."

Jada just wanted the process to go quickly so she could be at Cutty's side.

The police station was bustling with activity, and Jada was led into an interrogation room.

"Have a seat. Can I get you a water?" her driver asked.

Jada shook her head even though her mouth was dry, her tongue thick and immovable.

"I'll get some mug shots to see if you recognize anybody. You okay?"

Jada nodded, even though she wasn't, and the officer left her alone. Her stomach rolled as she looked down at her hands, still covered in Cutty's drying blood. *What if he dies?* Fresh tears sprang to her eyes, and she folded over her knees, gasping for air. *Have I even told him how I feel about him, or did I waste all our time together playing coy?* Images of Cutty flew through her mind, him wrapping the hands of the younger boys, stopping with a smile and encouragement for the older ones. *He's so good.* As the officer returned, Jada forced herself to wipe her eyes and sit up straight and tall.

Page after page of photographs filled the book, and Jada tried to find the two men's faces who had jumped them. She could see them clearly, but no matter how hard she tried, none of the photographs morphed into the men. An hour and a half later, she admitted defeat and pushed the book away. All the faces begun to blur together, and suddenly, she couldn't remember exact details from the two thugs because she had tried so hard to make them into one of the pictures.

"They're not in there." She sighed. "Could I have that water… something? I feel kind of shaky."

The officer, who had waited patiently without comment as she'd looked through the mug shots, nodded and left. When he returned, he had a bottle of apple juice. The tart taste of it on her tongue made her feel alive for the first time since they'd carted Cutty away.

"You think you can write a statement?"

"What does it need to say?"

"Whatever happened." He slid several sheets of paper across the table, and she picked up a pen.

She didn't want to think about it. She didn't want to relive the horrible moments when she'd been dragged into the nasty alley. She didn't want to think about when she'd realized Cutty had been stabbed. But she did it. She wrote everything she could remember and even wrote about the confrontation at the gym earlier in the week so the police would understand the attack wasn't random.

Jada was relieved to find Brodie and Chloe in the waiting area. They were both quick to hug her and inquire after her well-being.

"Have you heard how Cutty's doing?" Jada asked.

"Yeah, Levi texted me ten minutes ago. Cutty had X-rays and an MRI to check for organ damage," Brodie responded.

"Oh, I sure hope not!" Jada exclaimed. "Can we please go to Saint Agnes now?"

"Levi said it could take several hours, especially if the surgeon needs to repair something. I'm taking you home. You need your rest." It was well after midnight.

"Oh no, Brodie Parker, you are not taking me home. I'm going to be there for Cutty. I can sleep perfectly well in a chair beside his bed."

Brodie looked at Chloe for backup.

Jada was adamant. "If you take me home, I will walk to the hospital if I have to."

They exited the building and made their way over to the Smiths' car, where Michael waited.

"Saint Agnes," Brodie instructed him.

Jada recounted the attack as they drove to the hospital.

Chapter Eleven

"How is he?" Jada searched Levi's eyes after hugging him.

"He's resting. The doctor said surgery isn't necessary, as the scan showed no organ or intestinal damage," Levi replied.

"Thank God," Jada responded. "Can I sit with him, please?" She'd begged the charge nurse for permission to even be in Cutty's unit at such a late hour.

After sending Michael and Chloe home, Brodie had gone in search of coffee. They would need some sustenance to keep them going.

Jada entered the room quietly. Cutty's bed was the one closest to the door. His curtain had been mostly drawn to give him privacy and allow him time to sleep. He looked peaceful as he breathed slowly. A white blanket covered him up to his chest. Jada gently placed her hand on Cutty's arm, careful not to bump the intravenous line attached to him. His skin felt warm.

A nurse popped into Cutty's room. "Are you the girlfriend?" she asked, checking the monitors beside his bed. Short and plump, she wore tight yellow scrubs. Her white duty shoes squeaked as she maneuvered around the bed.

"Yeah, I'm Jada," she whispered.

The nurse walked to the wall opposite the bed. She erased some writing off the dry-erase board and wrote her name, Amy. "He's lucky. The knife wound could have been so much worse. We see this every day." Baltimore certainly had its share of violent crime, higher than the national average. "Planning on staying awhile?"

"As long as I can," Jada replied.

"Make yourself comfortable." Amy picked up a chair from under the board and set it beside Cutty's bed. "I'll wrangle a blanket for you."

"Thanks." Jada sat in the chair, grateful to spend some time alone with her man. The enormity of their situation finally began to hit home. She bowed her head and closed her eyes. *Thank you for sparing Cutty's life. Please help him recover. Let the police catch those guys who did this to us.* She closed with a barely audible, "Amen."

Before long, Jada heard a soft knock.

"Hey." It was Brodie standing at the door.

Jada stood and followed him into the large hallway.

He handed her a coffee and a packaged muffin. "Levi went home. Said he'll come back later in the day."

"Okay, I hope he gets some sleep." Jada took a sip of coffee. It was strong. She was touched that her cousin knew to add cream, just the way she liked it.

"He was able to get ahold of Cutty's parents. They're gonna drive here after breakfast."

"That's good. They must be worried sick." Jada felt for the older couple. It was such a long drive from Sneads Ferry.

"I found a blanket and a pillow," Amy said, returning as promised.

"That's so kind of you," Jada exclaimed. "This is my cousin, Brodie."

"Pleasure. You sticking around?" Amy sized him up.

"Yeah, if that's okay," Brodie replied politely.

"Jada can stay in the room... keep an eye on our patient. There's a lounge with a TV at the end of this hallway." Amy pointed, indicating the way. "You can rest on the sofa."

"Sounds good," Brodie replied.

He and Jada watched as Amy entered Cutty's room. She returned momentarily, free of the bedding.

"Let me know if the patient needs anything. There's a call button on the side of his bed." Amy addressed Jada. "He's on some pain meds. They make a person drowsy."

"Thanks." Jada was grateful.

"Mm-hmm." Amy walked away toward the nurse's station.

"I'll head to the lounge. Text me if you need anything."

"I will." Jada turned and headed back into Cutty's room.

"Dr. Naylor, please call Unit Twenty-Two. Dr. Naylor, Unit Twenty-Two." The female voice over the intercom was loud, waking Jada up.

It took a few seconds to get her bearings in the dimly lit room. Cutty was still sleeping—at least, his eyes were closed. She stretched her arms from underneath the cozy blanket, letting out a yawn. Her phone, still in silent mode, read 7:45. She wondered if Brodie was asleep down the hall.

"Hey, Sweet Pea. You been here long?" Cutty rubbed his eyes.

At the sound of his voice, Jada sprung out of her seat and carefully planted a kiss on Cutty's cheek.

"Mmmm, that's a nice way to start my morning." Cutty was cheerful, a good sign.

"I've been here since three-ish. How are you feeling?" Jada ran her fingers along the side of Cutty's head. He took hold of her hand and held it.

"A little groggy… and hungry. I'm sure they'll be servin' some breakfast soon." He sounded optimistic. "You okay? That punk grabbed you pretty hard." Cutty's eyes narrowed as he spoke of the incident.

"I'm fine, honestly." Jada tried to sound reassuring. "I spent hours looking at mug shots at the station last night, but I didn't see them. Then I wrote out my statement about the attack. And I included the incident at the gym." Talking about it gave her hair-raising vibes.

"Good, yeah… listen, Jada, you have to be aware of where you are at all times. Don't leave your house alone, and don't be out after dark."

"I won't. I promise." She studied his face for a moment. "The same goes for you." She couldn't imagine if something worse were to happen.

"Deal," Cutty replied.

The pair turned their attention to the door at the sound of a man pushing a large meal cart into the room.

"Good timing!" Cutty exclaimed.

"Good morning." The attendant put Cutty's bed into an upright position using foot controls. He then placed another pillow behind Cutty before setting the food tray on the side table. "Scrambled eggs, breakfast sausage, toast, apple juice, and coffee." The attendant listed off the items while slowly sliding the side table in front of Cutty.

"Sweet," Cutty replied.

The attendant walked around the curtain and began assisting Cutty's roommate.

"Looks delicious." Jada felt a little hungry herself. She hadn't touched her muffin yet. "I'll check on Brodie. He's down the hallway." She wanted to freshen up and give Cutty a few minutes alone to enjoy his breakfast.

Jada caught Brodie up to speed as they made their way to the cafeteria to purchase fresh coffee. When they returned to Cutty's room, they were greeted by the attending doctor. "Are you his family?"

"We're friends," Brodie was quick to reply.

"I'll be discharging Cutty this morning, as soon as the paperwork is complete," the doctor announced. "Will you be responsible for transporting him home?"

"Yeah, I'll call a cab," Brodie suggested.

"I'll text Elias," Cutty chimed in.

"Okay. Take it easy for the next few days." The doctor finished writing on his pad. He tore off the top sheet and handed it to Cutty. "A script for pain medication, if you need it. And follow up with your family doctor if you notice any change or discomfort at the site."

"Thanks, Doc," Cutty replied.

They watched as the doctor confidently strode out of the room.

"It'll be nice to be in my own bed, although everyone here has been so good to me." Cutty pushed the empty breakfast tray to the side.

"They probably need the bed for someone else, like, ASAP," Jada added.

"Did you get stitches?" Brodie asked curiously.

He had never seen a knife wound before, as far as Jada knew.

"A few." Cutty discreetly lifted his gown to show the wound. "It's not that long of a gash, but it went a little deep." The black sutures were evenly spaced over the dark-red tissue.

"Does it hurt?" Jada asked.

"Not really. They gave me something for pain last night, after the X-rays. And antibiotics to prevent infection." Cutty motioned to the IV bag.

"Glad you're okay, man," Brodie said, expressing his concern.

"Me too," Cutty agreed.

"Oh, sweet child," Ruby exclaimed as she hugged Jada at the door.

It was well after noon by the time Elias dropped Brodie and Jada off at home. Once they'd seen Cutty settled into his suite, a well-rested Levi took over the care of his friend. The boys were already planning a schedule for keeping the gym open under their supervision, giving Cutty respite.

"You must be starving." Ruby ushered them to the kitchen.

After washing their hands, the cousins sat at the table to eat the brunch Ruby had prepared.

"This is so fancy, Ma," Brodie exclaimed, ready to devour the delicious quiche, grits, bacon, and biscuits before him.

"I had to keep busy. I was worried about you all." Ruby looked at Jada. "But don't talk now. Just eat."

For the most part, Brodie had kept his mom up to date on the details as they'd unfolded via texting. After their meal, Jada headed upstairs to get some much-needed rest.

Ruby followed her to the bedroom. "I set out some pj's." She pointed to some shorts and a tank top on the bed.

Jada removed the sweatshirt Chloe had lent her at the police station. "Look at the bruising on your arms!" Ruby exclaimed. "What did they do to you?"

"One minute, Cutty and I were walking, then these guys got in our faces, the same guys at the gym on Friday." Jada realized it probably sounded confusing to her aunt, but she continued, "The short one grabbed me by my arms and pulled them tight behind my back. Cutty tried to protect me, but the other guy had a knife. I watched... helplessly." Jada recounted the events, from the quick arrival of the police and ambulance to her time at the police station. She felt drained reliving it all.

"Thank God you and Cutty are both safe." Ruby hugged her niece and tucked her into bed.

Chapter Twelve

MONDAY MORNING STARTED AS A good day after they all had better sleep than the previous night. Brodie headed off to work.

"I'll make shepherd's pie for Cutty and his parents," Ruby announced over breakfast. She had taken a break from quilting to keep an eye on her niece.

"What a great idea." Jada perked up. "I could bake them some muffins," she suggested.

"We have a few ripe bananas." Ruby pointed to the kitchen counter. "I'll dig out my recipe for banana oatmeal muffins. I like to add chocolate chips."

"Yum!" The muffins were a favorite of both Jada and Brodie.

The girls got down to business after clearing the dishes. Ruby made an extra casserole for dinner.

Around three in the afternoon, Jada and Ruby headed to the gym. People were out and about on the streets, and the traffic was picking up as it neared rush hour. Jada wore a pink sundress, as it was warm and sunny out. She admired the lovely mala bracelet on her wrist. Cutty had chosen well.

"On your toes, on your toes!" Levi's loud voice could be heard as the ladies entered the main entrance. He was watching ringside as two boys sparred.

"That's Levi." Jada pointed out Cutty's friend to her aunt.

Levi waved at the pair as they made their way to the suite.

"Cutty's lucky to have good friends," Ruby stated.

"He sure is." Jada's heart beat fast as she gently knocked. An older, white-haired man opened the door. Jada recognized him from Cutty's graduation picture.

"You must be Jada." His deep voice was authoritative yet welcoming as he clasped Jada's hand in both of his.

"Yeah, and this is my aunt Ruby," Jada replied.

"Marvin Jones, and my wife, Delores," he added, extending his arm back toward a middle-aged woman behind him.

"It's a pleasure to meet you both," Delores said. "I wish it was under different circumstances." She had the most beautiful wavy hair Jada had ever seen on an older woman. It was dark gray, sparsely infused with black, and she wore it rather stylishly, just below her ears. Jada instantly felt at ease with the couple, as they seemed down-to-earth and caring.

Ruby waved at Cutty, who sat upright in his bed. "We brought you all a little nourishment." Ruby placed the French white CorningWare on the kitchen counter.

"Ah, you ladies are spoiling us," Marvin exclaimed.

Jada followed suit and placed a platter of muffins covered in plastic wrap next to Ruby's large casserole dish. Then she turned toward Cutty and smiled. She slowly made her way over to him and carefully took a seat on the side of his bed. "How are you?" Jada searched Cutty's eyes. The indistinct chatter of their elders could be heard in the background.

"I'm hanging in there." Cutty looked a little tired. "What did you and your aunt make?"

"Aunt Ruby made shepherd's pie, and I made some banana oatmeal muffins with chocolate chips," Jada informed.

"That's so kind." Cutty's eyes opened wider as he noticed the bruising on her arm. "Did that punk do this to you?"

"Yeah. I'm okay," Jada shared. "I'm grateful it wasn't worse."

"That makes two of us," Cutty acknowledged.

"I hope they catch those thugs soon," Jada added. "I just want our lives to get back to normal."

"You are being careful, right?" Cutty inquired. "You aren't walking outside by yourself?"

"Yeah. So far, I've been out with Brodie and Aunt Ruby. But I don't expect them to go everywhere with me."

"Jada, listen to me." Cutty's voice was firm as he carefully took hold of her wrist. "Detective Walker stopped by last night. I told him about our interaction with those two guys at the gym on Friday morning."

"Ugh." Jada would rather forget it.

"The detective suspects those guys are part of a gang in the neighborhood."

"What?" Jada was shocked at first. "You know, that makes sense. The way they talked…" She shuddered, unable to finish her sentence.

"Right?" Cutty said. "The detective said someone from the police department would be in touch with you about looking at more photos to see if you can identify the attackers. I have to do the same once I feel better. And so do D'andre and Tyrell," Cutty added.

"Yeah, they would've had a good look at them on Friday," Jada agreed.

"It may have been a random attack—us bumping into them after the movie. But they have unfinished business with us." Cutty let the severity of his information sink in. "You need to be safe at all times, which means no walking outside by yourself. The reverend was just here, and he's coming up with a plan. He'll organize some people from the community to chaperone you as needed, especially once college starts, so that you aren't waiting at any bus stops by yourself. You should let campus security know as well, for when you stay late for cheer practice."

"Oh my goodness. That seems like a lot of trouble. I don't—"

"You don't have a say in this right now, Jada. Your safety is the priority. I mean, who knows what those punks would have done to you?" Cutty was serious.

"All right, Cutty," Jada conceded.

"And there's something else," Cutty added.

"Tell me." Jada was all ears.

"You can't come to the gym anymore, at least, not until these guys are caught."

Jada swallowed. She could hardly believe her ears. "You mean I can't work out here anymore? There's still time before school starts."

"I'm afraid not. The detective recommended it. Rev Joe and I both agree," Cutty stated. "If those punks show up, the boys will have my back. But I can't put you in harm's way."

Jada was taken aback. "What do you mean? I can't see you?"

"That's right, Jada. We can't be seen spending time together. It's for your safety. And it's for the best." Cutty's words were a bit harsh. He let go of her wrist. "You need to focus on your education now and your cheerleading squad."

"I see." It took all of Jada's strength to get her words out without breaking down in front of Cutty. It felt like he was dismissing her and their relationship. "So you know what's best for my safety and well-being." She stood. As Cutty didn't say anything further, she decided to leave while her dignity was still intact. "Take care of yourself." Jada bravely turned and walked toward the door.

"You too, Jada," was all Cutty said.

"It was nice meeting you both," Jada managed to say to Cutty's parents, holding back tears.

Ruby bade a quick farewell to Marvin and Delores and made her way to the door. By the time Ruby caught up to her, Jada was visibly crying. "Oh, sweetie," Ruby murmured.

Jada shook her head and waved her aunt off. It was a signal that she couldn't talk, at least, not right then. The two walked home together in silence. Once inside the town house, Jada headed upstairs and straight to her room.

Jada collapsed onto her bed and let the tears flow. She didn't want to look desperate in front of Cutty. *Does he realize how much I care about him?* She could hear his voice. *"We can't be seen spending time together." Maybe it's an excuse to break up with me.* His words at the gym haunted her, cut into her like the thug's knife. *Flippin' gangsters.* Anger coursed through her veins at the thought of those guys turning her and Cutty's lives upside down.

Breathe in, let the tummy expand—breathe out, let the tummy relax. Once her breathing cycle settled, she began to count her breaths. It helped, as the tears subsided. *Thank goodness for yoga,* as that was what she would do all week. No going for walks or to the gym for her. She would have to rely on YouTube videos for workout sessions until college and cheerleading practice started.

That was another reason she needed to keep it together. Since she'd received a full scholarship to college, she couldn't mess it up. She had to be strong and motivated for school, lest she let a few people down, including herself. *Who am I kidding?* Cutty was right when he told her to focus on her education and cheerleading. *How many people would love to be in my shoes right now? Minus the attack and breakup situation.*

The self-talk helped calm her down. *Perseverance.* That was what Rev Joe must mean when he preached about the tough times God's people endured. Jada recalled one of the reverend's sermons where he'd proclaimed such troubles were an opportunity for Christians to trust God, every day, and ask Him for the things they needed. So for the second time in two days, Jada bowed her head and said a prayer for Cutty and herself. Not only was she in need of spiritual nourishment, she was creating her sacred space.

Later that evening, Jada splashed a fair amount of cold water on her face before heading downstairs. She was hungry. It was time to face her aunt.

"Hi, sweetie. Ready to eat?" Ruby inquired as she watched television.

"Yeah. Smells good," Jada replied.

Ruby started to get out of her chair.

"Oh, don't get up, Aunty. I can serve myself."

Ruby remained seated while Jada took a serving of shepherd's pie and heated it in the microwave. Then she buttered a biscuit and poured herself a glass of water.

It reminded her of Cutty, since he'd encouraged her to drink more. She sat on the couch and slowly ate her supper while watching the news.

After she was finished eating, she complimented her aunt on the delicious supper. "I'm sure Cutty and his parents enjoyed it," Jada said courageously, but tears began to roll down her face.

Ruby stood and made her way to Jada's side. She rubbed her niece's back as Jada buried her head in her hands and leaned on the armrest. "What is it, sweetie?"

"Cutty told me I can't go to the gym anymore and that we can't be seen together. He said it's f-for my own safety." Jada tried to fight back the sobs, but it was no use.

"Aw. I'm sorry you have to go through this. Especially right before starting college," Ruby consoled. She continued to massage Jada's back. "I received a phone call from Reverend Joe tonight, explaining the chaperone system for you. At least until the police catch the attackers. You know Cutty has your best interests at heart."

"I don't get it," Jada admitted. "I mean, one minute, things were going so well between us, and the next thing I know, Cutty is ordering me to stay away. It's as if he's turning his back on our relationship."

"You know, Jada, I think this attack has really affected both of you, and your emotions are running high. Cutty could still be in shock, not to mention there could be side effects from the medication he's taking," Ruby said thoughtfully. "Give him time to heal. You'll see. I'm sure he'll miss you. Besides, he wants you to have a good start to your school year and not be burdened by all that has transpired."

"Oh, Aunty." Jada took a deep breath. "I sure hope you're right." Jada sat upright and turned her body so she could lay her head on Ruby's lap. Ruby continued to stroke Jada's head and shoulder.

"Your uncle Roy used to say, 'You grow through what you go through,'" Ruby shared.

"Hmmm," Jada responded.

They sat in silence for a while as the news continued on the television.

"Have you seen Brodie tonight?" Jada asked.

"Yeah, he stopped by earlier for a bite. Then he was helping Chloe take a grocery hamper to Cutty and his folks," Ruby replied. "The food was a gift from Chloe and Michael's parents. And I think Brodie was going to supervise at the gym for a bit this evening."

Hearing the news didn't make Jada cry. It felt comforting. Somehow, Aunt Ruby always knew the right thing to say.

Chapter Thirteen

"THANKS FOR COMING, DAD. IT means a lot." Cutty sat in the passenger seat of the spotless 2009 Chevy Blazer.

Marvin took pride in detailing his gray SUV. It was ingrained from maintaining fire engines throughout his career.

"All good," Marvin replied as he drove his son to the police station Wednesday morning. He knew the streets of Baltimore like the back of his hand.

After identifying himself at the front desk, Cutty was ushered into an interrogation room by an officer.

"Cutty, you're more mobile these days." It was Detective Walker who entered the room a few minutes later. He placed a stack of books on the desk.

"Hey, Detective." Cutty was pleasantly surprised to see a familiar face. "Here's my statement." He set a large manila envelope on the desk. He had written it the day before, while convalescing.

"All right, I'll take a look and pass it on to my team. Notify the staff at the front desk if you recognize anyone or if you have any questions." Detective Walker left Cutty to the arduous task of looking at mug shots.

Cutty had high hopes of identifying at least one of the attackers in the mug books, yet combing through page after page proved unsuccessful. *It must have been nerve-racking for Jada.* He wondered what she was up to that morning. It would be an adjustment for him, not seeing her at the gym. Her beautiful smile and graceful presence were welcome among the sweaty teenage boys. "Ahhhh." Cutty sighed in frustration.

"Just give it time," the attending officer at the front desk reassured Cutty. "One of those guys will slip up, and boom, he'll be in our data bank."

"It won't be soon enough," Cutty replied before heading outside to his dad's waiting vehicle. He just wanted the daunting ordeal to be over. It was time to focus on the gym and his tutoring proposal. *Time to get my head back in the game.*

"You're looking well." Cutty's supervisor, Linda, was on time for their scheduled meeting Thursday afternoon.

"My folks are taking good care of me." Cutty beamed with pride.

His parents had spent their morning tidying and cleaning the gym and his suite.

"I've received so much food from the community." His fridge and freezer were packed full.

"Fantastic," Linda replied. "It's commendable that you were able to keep the gym open while you were on holiday, and now this." She looked around the equipped space. The metal gleamed, with not a speck of dust in sight.

"Thanks to my buddies," Cutty responded. It was legit, as Linda had approved the substitute supervision roster prior to Cutty's departure.

"As for the other matter—" Linda paused. "I'm happy to say that your proposal has been approved."

"Yes!" Cutty raised his fists in jubilation. He'd had a feeling when he awoke that it would be accepted.

"Mr. Sykes was impressed with your plan, not to mention your qualifications."

Cutty smiled. "I'll make a poster and sign-up sheet for the bulletin board ASAP. Some of the boys may want to refresh the curriculum before school starts." The gears turned in Cutty's brain.

He and Linda spent a few minutes going over budget and funding matters. Before she left, Linda handed Cutty an envelope.

"What's this?" Cutty asked.

"Just a little something for you," Linda replied. "I'll stop by next month."

Once his supervisor exited the building, Cutty opened the envelope. He was touched to find a gift card to a local pizza parlor, along with well wishes. *Such a thoughtful gesture. I could invite Jada...* His heart sank as he resisted the urge to text her and share the good news.

She'd be ecstatic. But he had to stick to the plan and let Jada settle into college. It was for her safety. *I'll save it for a rainy day.* Cutty knew just the spot to put the gift card for safekeeping.

Jada accompanied her aunt to church on Sunday. It had been a while since she'd set foot in the sanctuary and listened to one of Rev Joe's sermons. She looked forward to it. She hoped to glean a sign of her future, possibly from the Scripture or, perhaps, by a chance encounter. At that point, Jada was open to anything. Being stuck at home had that effect on a person.

As she looked across the aisle, she saw the Smiths and waved. She was fortunate that Chloe had spent a couple of afternoons with her since Aunt Ruby had gone back to work. And Michael had given the girls a ride to the University of Baltimore so Jada could pick up her cheerleading uniform and the bulk of her textbooks. The girls helped one another choose their outfits for the first day of school. They watched movies and talked about the good old days.

"Are you still working out with Brodie?" Jada had the courage to ask.

"Yeah, he's pushing me. I miss working out with you," Chloe replied. "Did you know that Cutty's gonna be tutoring? He put up a poster..." Chloe stopped mid-sentence when she realized her faux pas. "Sorry, Jada."

"Yeah, I knew about his proposal. That's great." Jada felt a sudden pang in her heart.

D'andre and Tyrell had escorted Jada to the police station on Tuesday afternoon. They had each been notified to view mugs shots at the precinct, although separately, as a result of Cutty's conversation with Detective Walker during the previous Sunday. The threesome also gave details of the strangers from the gym to a sketch artist. But things took time. Jada was relieved to get that chore over with prior to college starting. And she was grateful for the boys' company.

"Recent events have challenged the ethos of our community," Rev Joe's voice boomed as he began his sermon. "Last month, a mother lost her son and a young boy lost his only brother." It wasn't news, yet emotional expressions could be heard throughout the pews. "And recently, a young couple was assaulted at knifepoint while walking home from the movie theater," the reverend continued. "Drugs are rampant in our beloved city. Every day, gang violence hits closer to home. People are afraid to walk the streets of Baltimore. Our government can put more money into law enforcement, but the police cannot stop drugs."

He had the attention of his congregation.

"What is the answer to stopping drugs?" The reverend looked over his flock. "It is found in the Word of God."

"Amen!" someone shouted.

"God can transform people when they put their trust and faith in Him." The reverend spent some time tying his message to Scripture and effortlessly brought his point home. "Look after one another. In other words, tend your garden while trusting in the Lord. Through these actions," he summed up, "good will prevail over evil." He closed his discourse in prayer.

Afterward, as Jada and Ruby stood to leave, the reverend approached them for a word. "Always nice to see you, ladies."

"You as well, Reverend," Jada responded.

"I really appreciated your message today, Reverend," Ruby added.

He smiled and nodded perceptively at Ruby.

"Let me know if you have any issues with the chaperones." The reverend had compiled a list of volunteers willing to help Jada and had given it to Ruby earlier in the week.

"Thank you. It must have taken a bit of work," Jada replied. "I've contacted campus security and will visit their office next week."

"Good." Rev Joe seemed satisfied. "You and Cutty are both in my prayers."

"Bless you," Ruby said warmly.

Jada just nodded. She didn't quite know what to say. Ruby took Jada's arm and walked her out of the sanctuary with composure.

"Have a good day," the elderly gentleman said as Jada boarded the bus on Wednesday morning. He was on the list of chaperones, mostly neighbors to the Parkers.

Jada felt mild anxiety as she prepared for her first day. It was hard to believe September had arrived.

Using a map of the University of Baltimore, Jada headed to her first class, a full-year English course. As she searched for a place to sit, someone tapped her arm softly.

"Hey, Jada." It was Olivia, from her cheerleading squad. "Want to sit together?"

"Hi, that would be great." Jada was relieved to see her new acquaintance. "I don't recognize a soul here." They chose a desk with two chairs near the front of the room and made themselves comfortable.

"How was your summer?" Olivia asked.

"Good. I went to Disney World with my family. And I worked out, tried to stay active." Jada was careful not mention anything about the attack, though she knew eventually, she would have to share some of the details. "How about you?"

"I got a job at an accounting firm, as an intern," Olivia replied cheerfully. "It was super busy."

After their second class, Introduction to Psychology, Olivia invited Jada to the food court. "I need some caffeine," Olivia announced. She headed toward the Starbucks.

Jada managed to find a table nearby. The girls nibbled away at their homemade sandwiches in silence.

"I can't wait for our first practice," Olivia announced as she opened a yogurt. It was scheduled for the next evening in the recreation center.

"Me too." Jada tried to sound enthusiastic, but she spotted Jamba Juice. *I wish Cutty was here, enjoying a banana-berry smoothie.*

"Everything okay?" Olivia asked, following her companion's forlorn gaze.

"Yeah." Jada forced a smile. "I have to run an errand. See you later?" She felt bad for deserting her new friend, but she had to get to campus security. It was time to take care of business.

Chapter Fourteen

CUTTY PUTTERED AROUND THE BOXING gym, assessing the equipment. It had been a little over a month since the attack, and he was feeling better. The gym was a little quiet that particular Thursday, since the boys were back in school. His stomach growled, reminding him that it was almost lunchtime. Suddenly, the front door swung open. Cutty turned to see Shondelle Jackson enter. Her son, Ricky, had been attending the gym since April. He was a polite, studious thirteen-year-old, and Cutty quite liked him.

"Hey, Cutty," Shondelle greeted him. "Look at you all up and about. I hope you aren't overdoing it."

"Hey, Shondelle," Cutty replied. "Nah, I'm just puttering around."

"Oh, good to hear. Ricky mentioned you're offering tutoring services." Shondelle approached Cutty and gave him a little hug. She was carrying a warm dish and a bag.

"That's right. I don't suspect Ricky needs my services."

"I reckon not. I never need to ask him if he's done his schoolwork. He's the epitome of an organized genius." Shondelle gave a little smile.

"Ah. What smells so good?" Cutty asked.

"It's a chicken casserole, my mom's recipe." Shondelle handed him the goods. "I made it this morning, along with some biscuits. Thought I'd drop it off on my way to work." Shondelle was a hairstylist and worked at a nearby salon.

"Aw, that's so nice of you!" Cutty exclaimed. "Your timing couldn't be better. I was just about to fix myself some lunch."

"Perfect." Shondelle smiled up at Cutty. She was an attractive single mom, a few years older than Cutty. She'd brought him a casserole before, back in the summertime. "How are you feeling?"

"Better. I've started working out again." Cutty couldn't help but smile back at her.

"Well, I'm glad. Ricky and his friends talk about you all the time," she added. "You are quite the hero to the young boys."

Cutty shook his head. "I don't know about that. I'm just trying to keep a low profile, hoping that things get back to normal soon."

"And you're doing a fine job of that," Shondelle praised him. She placed a hand on Cutty's left forearm while handing him her business card with her free hand. "Please call or text me if you ever need help with anything," she said sincerely.

"Thanks. I really appreciate the food. I'll bet it's delicious."

"My pleasure," Shondelle replied. "I should be going now. I have a client booked at noon."

"Yeah, no worries," Cutty said. "Take care."

He watched as Shondelle waved then turned and made her way to the door.

Cutty let out a little sigh as he headed toward his suite. *There's no shortage of good eats and pretty faces.* After eating the tasty casserole, Cutty took a short nap. His buddy Levi was going to supervise the boxing gym after four, when it was sure to be busy. Besides, Cutty had an important engagement at four thirty. Rev Joe was bringing the late Devon Lewis's family, Clarice and Davey, over to meet Cutty and tour the gym. Since Cutty was feeling better, he felt it was time to look in on Devon's family and offer his support.

Levi arrived at the boxing gym a few minutes early. Cutty was happy to see his friend. "Hey, buddy."

The two men hugged.

"How's it going?" Levi asked.

"Good. Ricky's mom dropped off a casserole and biscuits earlier. They were amazing," Cutty shared enthusiastically.

"Sweet. Any leftovers?" Levi asked.

"Help yourself. I'll spell you off for supper later," Cutty offered.

"Will do. I'd better get to work." Levi headed toward the boxing ring as a few boys began wrapping their wrists.

Cutty felt grateful. Feeding Levi was the least he could do to repay his friend. Cutty remembered a time when Levi had needed assistance in his struggle with addiction. Elias and Cutty had been relentless in their support for Levi. Though, ultimately, it was Levi who needed to want to get better and take the necessary steps, it was a process. But seeing all that Levi had accomplished over the recent years had been an affirmation to his friends. And experiencing the karma as Levi helped Cutty was a bonus.

The reverend walked into the gym at four thirty, as arranged, with Clarice and Davey in tow. He made the necessary introductions to Cutty.

"It's nice to finally meet you both." Cutty shook their hands.

"Likewise," Clarice answered. She was in her midthirties and had a polite yet sad aura about her.

Davey took in his surroundings, from the workout equipment to the boxing ring, where Levi was busy coaching some boys.

"I can't tell you how sorry I was to learn about your son's passing back in July," Cutty continued. He kept his composure genuine and focused as he spoke. "Such a senseless tragedy. I wish I had met Devon. I don't believe he ever visited the boxing gym."

"Yeah, my Devon wasn't much for organized stuff. He liked to be a little wild. I wish he'd found this place. It might have given him a release." Clarice put her arm around Davey's shoulders and drew him close for a second. "Davey's been looking forward to coming here since the reverend mentioned it last week."

"Glad to hear that," Cutty replied. "Davey, how about I show you around the gym and introduce you to some of the boys here?"

"Okay." Davey nodded.

Cutty placed his left hand on Davey's shoulder and gently steered him toward the boxing ring. The first stop was introducing Davey to Levi and the boys under his supervision. They spent a few minutes watching the boys spar. Cutty explained to Davey what was happening in the ring. After a while, Cutty showed Davey around the rest of the gym, explaining about the cardio equipment, weights, and punching bags, ending with a quick look into the men's changing room. The last thing Cutty showed Davey was the bulletin board, which was well organized. He talked a little about the tutoring services. The poster about Devon was still at the center of the board.

By the time Cutty brought Davey back to his mom, it was settled. Davey would return to the gym the next day after school and begin some boxing training. Clarice shook Cutty's hand before placing her arm around Davey.

"Thanks, Cutty. I'll be in touch with you soon. Take it easy," the reverend stated before escorting the Lewis family home.

Later that evening, Cutty was able to give Levi a supper break.

After thirty minutes had passed, Levi returned to the boxing gym. "Thanks for supper. It was delicious."

"*Mi casa es su casa*," Cutty replied.

He and Levi chuckled at the popular Spanish phrase, which literally meant, "My house is your house." Levi resumed his supervision of the boys sparring in the boxing ring while Cutty went over some ninth-grade math with one of the boys.

At seven forty, the main door slammed shut. Cutty glanced over to find D'andre headed in his direction. Cutty knew something was up, as he could feel the energy bouncing off D'andre.

"What's up, my friend?" Cutty inquired.

"You'll never believe it," D'andre exclaimed. He was slightly winded. "I was walking by the gas station, not five blocks from here, when I spotted this dark-colored SUV. I wouldn't have given it a second look, except I noticed the guy pumping gas into it. He was short... kind of reminded me of those dudes who were messin' with you and Jada."

"Go on," Cutty urged, listening carefully.

"Yeah. I was fairly certain it was the same guy. So I backtracked and went inside the convenience store.

When I looked at the SUV again, I noticed the tall guy sitting in the front passenger's seat."

Cutty's blood boiled at the thought of those punks.

"I knew I had to act or I'd miss the opportunity to get a picture of those dudes. So I filmed them on my phone."

"Say what?" Cutty was concerned. If they were the same two thugs who had attacked him and Jada, then they were dangerous.

D'andre held up his iPhone and grinned at Cutty. "That's right, boss. I got it all right here, even the license plate number."

"That's huge. But you have to be careful, D'andre. Don't share this information with anyone other than the police."

"I won't. You never know who might associate with them," D'andre added. "I came straight to the gym to show you." D'andre played the video for Cutty.

After watching, Cutty was convinced they were the two guys who'd visited the gym back in August. His mood went from anger to jubilation at the thought of being one step closer to identifying the thugs. "I'll call Detective Walker." Cutty looked thoughtful. "Follow me to my suite." The last thing he wanted was to unsettle the boys.

"Most definitely," D'andre agreed.

Cutty asked Levi to close the gym, as it was almost eight. Once they were in the privacy of his suite, Cutty dialed the detective's number and hit Speaker.

"Detective Walker," he answered on the third ring.

"It's Cutty, from the gym. One of the boys saw my attackers tonight. He's got them on video with his phone, license plate and all."

"Bingo," Detective Walker responded. "Can you and your buddy come down to the station now?"

D'andre nodded.

"Yeah, we can," Cutty replied, giving a thumbs-up.

After ending the call, Cutty updated Levi on their situation before heading to the station with D'andre. The thought of getting those punks off the street gave Cutty hope. Living in limbo wasn't easy. *I could ask Jada out properly.*

Chapter Fifteen

"HELLO?" JADA ANSWERED HER iPHONE. She sat near the front of the bus on her way to school.

"Is this Jada?"

"Speaking." Jada tried to place the deep male voice.

"This is Detective Tommy Walker with Baltimore Homicide."

"Yes?" Jada recalled meeting him in the gym at the beginning of the summer. But it was October 27. *Is this about Devon's murder?*

"The police have detained and formally charged two men suspected of murdering Devon Lewis." Detective Walker paused before continuing, "They are the same pair that assaulted you and Cutty in August."

"What?" Jada gasped. "How?" She was speechless.

"As it is an ongoing investigation, I can't divulge all the details just yet. Suffice to say that the Baltimore Police Department has received tips and video surveillance from multiple sources."

"Oh my goodness, this is good news, right?" Jada asked.

"That's correct. You can safely resume your daily activities," Detective Walker replied. "You'll need to call the station and arrange a visit to identify the perpetrators. The sooner, the better."

"Okay, I'll do that this morning." Her head spun with ideas. She would let campus security know and tell the reverend she no longer needed chaperones. "Thank you, Detective." Jada was relieved as she ended the call.

Cutty must know already. She sincerely hoped he would find comfort in knowing Devon's murder had finally been solved, as it had troubled Cutty so deeply from the beginning. She wondered what it would mean for her and Cutty. *Will he contact me?* Perhaps he had met someone else. He was only human, after all.

"Your text this morning made my day," Chloe shared as she waited for her tea to cool. She'd agreed to meet Jada at Starbucks after classes finished for the day.

"My aunt will finally get a decent sleep." Jada had also texted Ruby and Brodie the news once she'd ended the call with the detective. She took a bite of her oat fudge bar. She couldn't remember the last time she'd had a coffee date with her friend. Freedom tasted good.

"I am so relieved now that those thugs have been arrested," Chloe said. "Michael and I've been careful ever since you and Cutty were attacked."

"Geez, Chloe, I didn't even think about that. I've been so wrapped up in my own world," Jada confessed. "I wonder how Devon's family is doing."

"It must be bittersweet for them," Chloe replied. "I hope the police lock up the criminals and throw away the key."

Jada admired her friend's perceptiveness. "I've missed this." She pointed toward Chloe then back at herself.

"Me too." Chloe smiled wistfully before adding, "You should come to the Halloween party this Friday night at the gym."

"Oh?" Jada responded.

"Yeah. Cutty's putting it on for the boys. Brodie, Michael, and I are helping with setup and supervision."

Jada was intrigued. "Our campus is hosting an exhibition game Friday night, so I'll be busy cheerleading. And there's a big hall party afterward. I'll see how I feel after the game. Please don't say anything to the guys. Let me think about this one."

"Gotcha," Chloe replied knowingly.

"We did it!" Olivia high-fived Jada as they entered the girls' locker room. "I messed up on the last routine."

"I slipped near the beginning, after my first jump," Jada shared. "Probably no one even noticed. Did you hear the crowd?" The school spirit was high as the University of Baltimore's basketball team won their first game by a close margin.

"They were full of energy," Olivia replied. "Hey, are you coming to the after-party?" she asked as Jada grabbed her belongings out of the locker.

"Not this time. I'm sure you'll have fun." Jada winked at her friend since Olivia had recently expressed interest in the eligible athletes. "See you." Jada made a quick exit and headed for the bus stop.

Hey, girl, are you coming?! The place looks insane! The text was from Chloe.

Yup. On my way! Jada typed. She locked the front door of her town house and began walking toward the gym. At sixty-eight degrees, the weather was uncharacteristically warm. She was still wearing her cheerleading attire. It would have to suffice as a costume.

As Jada neared the entrance, the nervous energy that had lingered inside her all day ramped up. *Does Cutty even want me here?* She was about to change her mind and go back home, when the door opened, and out walked Tyrell and D'andre.

"Hey, Jada, long time no see," D'andre exclaimed.

"Damn, girl, you're looking fine tonight," Tyrell said.

"It's been way too long." Jada hugged each of the boys. They'd probably never even seen a cheerleader up close before. "Nice costumes."

Clad in satin shorts and one boxing glove each, the boys looked the part of professional boxers.

"Are you leaving?"

"No, just getting some air." D'andre nodded toward the gym. "Save me a dance?"

"Of course. See you later," Jada responded.

As she reached for the door, two teenage girls emerged, giggling. They appeared to be in pursuit of the boys. Jada smiled. Encountering Tyrell and D'andre had been the confidence boost she'd needed.

The sound of pop dance music reverberated as Jada entered the gym. She stood for a moment, taking in the sight. Cutty and his tribe had really outdone themselves, transforming the gym into a Halloween nightclub. Not only was the place filled with decorations, but a strobe light had been installed above the dance floor, formerly the open space of the gym. Jada spotted Brodie and Chloe dancing together. Off to one side, Michael talked to some teenagers, all of whom were in costume. They stood next to a generously laden snack and beverage table.

Wow, what a great experience for the kids.

When Jada turned and looked toward the cardio equipment, her heart skipped a beat. There stood Cutty, along with Levi. Cutty's face broke into a smile when their eyes met. He carefully made his way toward her, dodging a few excited partygoers.

"Look who's here!" Cutty gave her a hug then stepped back to examine her outfit.

Jada's getup consisted of a purple miniskirt and a matching cropped long-sleeved top, which bore the

University of Baltimore's logo. Her outfit was complete with white tennis shoes and ankle socks.

"You look amazing." His eyes shone with genuine interest.

"Thanks. I just came from an exhibition game at the university. You don't look too bad yourself." Jada assumed he was dressed up as Sinbad, as he wore white baggy pants with a red sash, an open black vest with no shirt, a small gold turban, and a gold band on his upper left arm. She was pleased to see he hadn't shaved his beard.

"Who won?" Cutty asked.

"Our team. They were playing against the University of Maryland. It was pretty tense."

"Oh, fantastic. You should be out celebrating with your team tonight."

"Yeah, I took a rain check. I figured I was overdue to see everyone here, since the safety ban was lifted. You've done a great job of setting up the gym in the spirit of Halloween." Jada's praise was heartfelt.

Cutty grinned. "Thanks, Jada. But I can't take all the credit. Brodie, Michael, and Chloe were in charge of the decorations. I set a budget, and as you can see, they did a fine job." Cutty motioned his arm around the gym. "The Smiths supplied the snacks and drinks."

"That's so sweet of them." Jada beamed.

Chloe and Michael's parents were very generous.

Just then, D'andre walked up to the pair. "Ready for that dance?"

"Sure." Jada headed to the dance floor with mixed emotions. Her conversation with Cutty was going well, but she'd promised D'andre earlier. She loved dancing. *Time to show these guys some moves.*

It turned out D'andre was a pretty good dancer also. When the song ended, he escorted Jada to the side. "Tyrell and I set up the strobe light."

"Cool," Jada replied.

Chloe and Brodie approached them.

"Nice moves," Chloe complimented.

The boys began chatting.

"How's it going?" Cloe asked her friend.

"Well, I'm glad I came." Jada smiled.

Before long, the teens in attendance started leaving the party, as their curfew was ten thirty. A few parents arrived to escort some of the youths home. Cutty received many fist bumps and handshakes as people said their goodbyes and thank-yous.

Brodie, Chloe, and Michael cleaned up some. After assuring Cutty they would be back midmorning to take down the decorations, they left the gym.

Jada was left alone with Cutty. She made herself useful by helping him carry leftover food into his suite. They consolidated the snacks and put them into the refrigerator. Jada carefully washed the punch bowl Mrs. Smith had donated.

Cutty made a final round of the gym and locked it up before returning to his suite. "Thanks for washing those dishes. I'm a little scared to touch the fine glassware."

"I'm happy to help." Jada smiled.

"Do you have a few minutes to talk? I can walk you to your town house."

Jada nodded. "Yeah, let's talk."

Cutty led her to the sofa. "I was so relieved to hear the news from Detective Walker. It's a miracle the police caught those thugs." His tone was serious.

"I feel the same. How is Devon's family?"

"They've had rough days, for sure. Davey works out here after school, and I'm tutoring him in math and English."

"Aw, I had no idea." Jada's heart nearly burst with pride. She admired Cutty's willingness to encourage the youth to see their potential. "Have the police said why Devon was murdered?"

"They suspect it was retaliation for a territorial dispute. The narcotics unit has been investigating the responsible gangs for some time. Their empires are being disrupted. But I never expected Devon's murderers to be the same two punks who attacked us." Cutty paused briefly. "How are you coping? I bet your classes and cheering keep you busy. Everyone kind of kept me informed. Brodie said you took a self-defence class. How was that?"

"The self-defence course was helpful. School has definitely kept me on my toes. But I have to admit that being here tonight reminds me how much I've missed the boys and the gym." Jada paused then added, "I've missed you too, Cutty."

Cutty smiled. He placed his hand on top of Jada's.

"Can I see your scar?" Jada asked softly.

Cutty pulled his vest to the right to reveal the two-inch knife-wound scar close to his waist.

Jada gingerly touched it. As she withdrew her fingers, Cutty placed his hand under Jada's chin and kissed her. It was soft and sensual at first. Feeling the intensity of his lips gave her clarity like never before.

"Mmmm… that was nice," Cutty murmured as they slowly broke apart. "I've missed you too."

"Have you, now?" Jada purred.

"Mm-hmm. I should probably walk you home."

"Would it be all right if I spent the night here?" Jada asked. "I mean, we can just cuddle."

Cutty looked surprised. "What about your aunt?"

"Aunt Ruby's gone to Newark for the weekend. She's visiting her cousin Sally."

Cutty hesitated. He didn't look convinced.

"Unless you've met someone else." Jada felt silly for assuming Cutty was unattached.

"No." Cutty shook his head. "There's no one else. How about you? Have any of those handsome basketball all-star players wangled you out on a date yet?" he teased.

"Nah. I haven't had time." Jada giggled. *Nor a desire, for that matter.*

They both smiled.

"It's good seeing you. I don't want our visit to end." Jada was determined. "I'll sleep in my uniform," she pleaded softly.

"All right, shawty," Cutty relented.

Jada freshened up first. When she came out, Cutty had changed into some pajama shorts and a muscle shirt. After his turn in the bathroom, he charged his iPhone and turned off the lights. Jada followed him to his bed.

Cutty pulled aside the soft duvet. "Ladies first."

Jada slid to the middle of the queen-size bed. It felt enormous. Cutty lay on his side, facing Jada, so she turned her back toward him and snuggled close.

He played with her hair some, inhaling the scent. His breath was warm on the back of her head as he exhaled. She loved feeling the thud of his heart through his ribcage. His hand left her tresses and rested on her shoulder momentarily before gently stroking the length of her arm. His touch sent shivers across her skin.

Jada turned back a little, her free hand clasping his. As they interlaced their fingers, she felt physically connected to Cutty. After weeks of separation, her dream of being his girl seemed a realistic possibility.

Cutty gently kissed the back of Jada's head. "Good night."

"Sweet dreams," Jada murmured.

Jada woke to the smell of bacon frying. Cutty stood by the stove, holding a spatula.

"It smells divine." Jada clenched her fists and stretched, savoring the scenery as well as the aroma.

"Good morning, shawty. Would you like some orange juice?"

"I'd love some." Jada popped into the washroom then sat at the table. Cutty placed two plates of scrambled eggs, bacon, and sliced tomatoes before them.

"These eggs are delicious. I like that you added peppers," Jada praised, hungry since she hadn't eaten much the previous evening.

"Thanks. Any plans for today?"

"I have an English paper due on Wednesday, so I'll be working on that from home. And I should probably do some laundry. Will the gym be open today?"

"Yes, after the party decor is cleaned up," Cutty answered.

"Oh, right, the cleaning crew are helping you later this morning. I guess I should get going, then." Jada grinned. After she cleared the table, Cutty walked Jada to the back door of his suite, which opened to the alley.

"If you aren't busy tonight, would you like to hang out and watch a movie?"

"Yeah, that could work. Thanks for breakfast." Jada gave him a hug.

"See you later," Cutty replied.

Later that evening, Jada arrived at Cutty's back door. "Hey."

"Hey yourself," Cutty answered. "Nice jeans." Jada wore ripped skinny jeans with a mauve blouse. She'd grabbed a black moto jacket at the last minute, as the temperature had dropped slightly.

"Thanks." She liked that he noticed. "How was your day?"

"It was surprisingly busy in the gym. But I managed to sneak in a little nap after closing."

"Aw, good for you. I did the same after working on my paper," Jada added. "What are we watching tonight?"

"Would you be up for *The Wolverine*? It's an action movie starring Hugh Jackman. Have you seen it?"

"No, that's sounds fine. Anything will be a distraction from schoolwork."

Cutty set out some snacks left over from the party, and the pair sat down on the sofa to watch their movie.

Afterward, Jada helped carry the dishes to the sink. "Well, that was entertaining."

"Yeah, not too bad," Cutty agreed. "It received some mixed reviews. At least the superhero stayed true to the comic. Jackman really inhabited the role."

Jada was impressed by his knowledge. Cutty connected his iPhone to a Bluetooth speaker and shuffled through his playlist. Then he sat on the sofa.

Jada walked over to the couch and sat facing Cutty. "Are you tired?"

"Not really," Cutty replied. "You?"

Jada shook her head no. They looked at each other, and Jada tipped her head toward Cutty and placed her lips on his. Cutty pulled her fully into a kiss. Jada's lips sought his softly. As their kiss lingered, she rested her hands on his chest then slowly began to glide her hands over his muscular upper body.

"You smell so good," Cutty uttered softly as they slowly parted.

Jada looked up at him tentatively. "Will you lie with me tonight?" she whispered.

"Jada, I... I don't have any protection." Cutty appeared caught off guard.

"We don't need protection, not tonight."

Cutty's confusion showed on his face.

"Back in August, when things were ramping up between us, I asked my doctor for a birth control prescription," Jada explained quietly. She'd taken them regularly ever since. "It's all good." She kissed him again. When they broke apart, Jada stood and took Cutty by the hand, steely determination in her eyes.

"Well then," Cutty stated. He followed as Jada led him to his side of the bed. She took off her blouse then helped him take off his T-shirt. Next, she undid her jeans and slipped out of them. Cutty followed suit.

Rhythm and blues played from his iTunes as they stood facing each other. Jada's heart skipped a beat when Cutty touched her lilac-colored lace push-up bra, caressing the exposed skin beneath her décolletage. When his finger dropped to her belly bling, Jada held her breath.

He gently toyed with the large rhinestone butterfly. "I've never seen one up close before," he murmured. Cutty carefully placed his two thumbs inside Jada's matching lace hipsters and slid them down her legs.

When her panties hit the floor, Jada undid her bra and took it off.

"You're so beautiful." Cutty cupped her breasts with both hands.

Jada felt warm and fuzzy as the love hormone entered her bloodstream.

When Cutty removed his boxers, Jada was enthralled by his arousal. Eager to keep things progressing, she turned and pulled back the covers. Cutty's eyes were alight with desire as they lay facing one another. Jada was thirsty for him as he stroked her jaw with his thumb and caressed her neck and shoulders.

His mouth found her breast. A sensual feeling seared throughout Jada as his kiss turned into a tug, first on one then the other. She ran her fingers through his hair, not wanting the feeling to end. Cutty's mouth traveled down her abdomen and finally paused between her legs as he positioned his body at the end of the bed. His breath was warm on her skin as he kissed her and exquisitely maneuvered his tongue. Jada felt exposed yet barely self-conscious as new sensations overcame her.

"Oh, Cutty," Jada cried. She arched her back as the warmth of a thousand suns coursed through her body. Cutty kissed her inner thigh.

A moment later, he was on top of her. Once again, his hand stroked her neck. Then, with all the tenderness Cutty possessed in that moment, he entered her.

Afterward, as they lay entwined, Jada looked into his eyes. "I love you."

"I love you too, Sweet Pea," Cutty replied before kissing her leisurely.

The endearing term made Jada shed a few tears. She was happy beyond measure. With his thumb, Cutty gently wiped the moisture from the side of her face. Jada watched his face for a while once his eyes were closed. It didn't take long for the rhythm of his breathing to slow.

For the second morning in a row, Jada woke to the smell of breakfast cooking. "What's on the menu today?"

"It's oatmeal for the young lady," Cutty replied teasingly.

"Do you have any brown sugar?" she asked.

"I sure do," he answered.

"Perfect." Jada slipped into her clothes. After freshening up, she found Cutty standing beside his bed.

He seemed deep in thought as she approached him. "There's blood on the sheets. Jada, did I hurt you last night?" Cutty looked concerned.

Jada realized what he was noticing. "Oh, no... I'm fine. I read once that this sometimes happens to a girl after her first time." She smiled reassuringly.

"Oh. I was worried." Cutty sighed gratefully as he hugged Jada.

Jada looked up into Cutty's eyes. "How did you learn about making love?"

Cutty drew a long breath before replying, "I suppose I heard some talk in the locker rooms, but you can't believe everything you hear. And I've dated a couple of girls, but no one recently."

Jada smiled wistfully. "Can we eat now, please? I'm starving," she gently prodded Cutty.

"Absolutely." He led Jada to the table.

Chapter Sixteen

"WOULD YOU LIKE THESE WRAPPED?" the salesclerk asked Cutty.

"Yeah, thanks." After paying for the bouquet, Cutty walked to the bus stop. *Flowers for my girl.* He planned on surprising Jada, as her cheer squad was performing. It was Wednesday, November 5, and the University of Baltimore men's basketball team was hosting their season opener against the Towson University Tigers.

Once he arrived at the recreation center, Cutty found a seat in the bleachers and tucked the bouquet safely underneath. Loud music roared from the speakers as the cheerleaders made their way to the court.

"Here we go!" someone yelled.

Cutty was awestruck by Jada and her squad. Not only were they confident and energetic, but they worked well together as they performed to the hip-hop mix. The crowd was amped when the players from both teams emerged. Everyone stood for the national anthem.

I'll have to do this more often. Cutty couldn't re-member the last time he'd been to a varsity game. The

University of Baltimore erased a seven-point halftime deficit to beat the Towson Tigers seventy to sixty-four.

Cutty wasn't sure if Jada saw him in the stands, so he walked over, close to where she stood, just prior to the girls heading into their locker room after the finale. "Hey, Jada." He waved at her.

She looked up and waved excitedly at him. "I'll be ten minutes," Jada informed him then disappeared with her squad.

When Jada reappeared, she had changed into some black leggings, a purple blouse, black flats, and a cropped denim jacket. Her hair was curled and had a thin braid running above her forehead. The squad tried to coordinate their hair styles to match one another, she said. "What a nice surprise! Did you enjoy the game?" she asked, giving Cutty a big hug.

"I sure did. Baltimore played well tonight," he replied. "And what a show you and your squad put on. You girls rocked!"

"Aw, thanks." Jada beamed. "They're a great bunch, and we have so much fun."

"It shows," Cutty praised. "Here, these are for you." He handed Jada the flowers wrapped in some floral paper.

"Oh, how sweet." Jada graciously accepted the bouquet but would open it later. "Did you ride the bus here?"

"Yes," Cutty answered. "Can I escort you home?"

"That would be lovely."

The pair headed out of the recreation center and made their way to the bus stop.

"This feels like déjà vu," Jada noted, referring to the time Cutty had escorted her to tryouts.

"It sure does," Cutty agreed.

They shared how their week had been going. Within about five minutes, their bus arrived.

"After you, Sweet Pea." Cutty motioned for Jada to board before him.

She chose a window seat near the middle of the bus, and Cutty sat beside her. As the bus made its way off campus, Jada peeled back a part of the floral paper.

She seemed delighted at the dozen red roses surrounded by white baby's breath. "Oh, Cutty, they're gorgeous!" Jada exclaimed, and she breathed in their intoxicating scent.

"I'm glad you like them," Cutty said softly.

Jada looked adoringly into Cutty's eyes and kissed him.

Jada and her family celebrated Cutty's birthday with him on Sunday, December 7, with a delicious roast beef supper Ruby prepared.

"On the count of three," Jada ordered the guests as she set two chocolate cupcakes topped with strawberry icing in front of Cutty and lit the candles. "One, two, three."

The guests, including Brodie, Chloe, Michael, Levi, and Rev Joe, all sang "Happy Birthday" to their friend. Ruby served them all individual cupcakes and tea for herself and the reverend.

"Thank you all for making my twenty-fifth special." Cutty was touched.

"How's the tutoring program going?" the reverend asked while the ladies cleared the dishes.

"It's going well," Cutty replied. "Word is spreading, so every week, more boys approach me for help." Attendance was busier. "I couldn't do it without Levi's help."

His buddy had spent more time volunteering at the gym.

"It's rewarding. Plus, I get in a regular workout," Levi commented.

"Once the kids get through the first semester and see their marks, I'll have a better idea of how effective my strategies have been," Cutty added.

"Our community is blessed to have you both," the reverend praised.

Afterward, when the couple spent some time alone together in Cutty's suite, Jada presented him with a birthday card. Inside, Cutty was blown away to discover two tickets for a concert featuring the Weeknd. It was scheduled for late spring of 2015 in Washington, DC.

"What a great surprise. I don't even know what to say." Cutty was stoked.

"It'll be my first concert," Jada shared. "We can buy matching T-shirts."

"Something to look forward to." Cutty took Jada in his arms.

"That was the best brunch I've ever had," Cutty complimented his hostess.

Ruby had outdone herself with an egg, ham, and cheese casserole accompanied by a fruit platter. Jada had baked blueberry white-chocolate scones for the occasion.

"I'm glad you were able to spend Christmas with us," Ruby replied.

It was fitting to invite Cutty, since he'd kept the gym open during winter break. It gave the boys a much-needed outlet for their energy.

"Shall we open gifts?" Brodie asked. He was eager to head to the Smiths' house and hang out with Chloe.

"I'll go first." Jada handed Cutty a gift bag. Inside was an olive-green hoodie and a water bottle, both from Lululemon. "There's more." She passed him a flat box.

"Oh, it's perfect," Cutty exclaimed as he unwrapped a twelve-month planner for 2015.

"It has space to journal," Jada pointed out, as she knew Cutty liked to create programs for the gym.

"Thanks, Sweet Pea." Cutty passed her a gift bag.

"Mmmm." Jada held a pink bath bomb to her nose and inhaled. "Just what I need to relax from studying."

She extracted an array of spa items, including bubble bath and soap.

Cutty waited patiently, a smile on his face, before handing her a small box with a silver bow on top.

It took Jada a minute to unwrap it, as it was sealed well with tape. "They're gorgeous!" she exclaimed as she held up a pair of white-gold hoop earrings with tiny diamonds.

"Lovely," Ruby said after Jada passed them to her.

Cutty gave Ruby a cookbook from Sneads Ferry and a gift card to Macy's. And for Brodie, he bought a Baltimore Orioles baseball jersey. Brodie gave Cutty movie passes and a gift card to a local restaurant.

It was Ruby's gift to Cutty that stole the show. She handed him a large box wrapped in red Christmas paper. Cutty opened the box carefully. He was a little self-conscious about opening the largest gift in the room. He slowly pulled out a queen-size quilt, the one Ruby had been working on during the summer. He held it up to display a large, centered earth in multiple shades of green with an off-white background. Across the bottom of the quilt, Ruby had hand stitched the words *Your Presence on This Earth Makes a Difference*. Cutty was speechless. He stood, walked to where Ruby sat, and gave her the biggest hug.

"This is a pretty special gift, Ruby. I can't imagine how many hours you put into making it," Cutty said.

"It was a labor of love," Ruby stated. "I think about all the hours you put into our community and how well you treat my niece and my son. You make a difference in people's lives, and I don't ever want you to forget that."

Jada teared up a bit as she hugged her aunt. "All that time I saw you working on this quilt, and I had no idea it was for Cutty."

"I know how to keep a secret." Ruby chuckled.

"You're the bomb, Cutty." Brodie fist-bumped Cutty. It was a pretty amazing moment, as it summed up the feelings shared within the household.

Saturday, January 3, 2015, was Jada's nineteenth birthday. Cutty treated Jada, Brodie, Chloe, and Ruby to supper out at his favorite Mexican restaurant, the Blue Agave. Ruby had offered to cook, but Cutty wanted to give her a break, since she had cooked so much over the holidays. It was his way of thanking Jada's family for all their generosity.

Later that evening, while visiting his suite, Jada opened the birthday card from Cutty. Inside was a gift card for a spa. Jada was impressed. However, she didn't recognize the name of the business.

"It's in the Westin Hotel, in downtown Washington, DC," Cutty announced.

Jada looked a little perplexed.

"I'll be attending a conference there in February. Actually, it's on Valentine's Day weekend," Cutty furthered. "I was hoping you would join me."

"Oh, that sounds lovely," Jada said.

"I asked your aunt for permission, and she gave me her blessing," Cutty shared. He had a gleam in his eye.

"That's awesome. I guess it's settled, then." Jada grinned. "You'll be in a conference, and I'll be getting pampered." She waved the gift certificate in front of Cutty's face.

"Yes, and there's a dinner and dance that Saturday evening, so you'll need to bring a dress," Cutty stated.

"Sounds fancy." Jada was excited. "It'll be an excuse for Chloe and me to go shopping. We really need some retail therapy."

Jada texted Chloe asking about a good time for the two to meet up.

Chapter Seventeen

CUTTY AND JADA TAXIED TO Camden Station, where they boarded an afternoon train on Friday, February 13. The commuter train ride took approximately one hour, and the couple disembarked at Union Station in Washington.

"This is gorgeous!" Jada exclaimed as she took in the architecture.

The main hall, modeled after the Baths of Diocletian in Rome, featured white marble floors, barrel-vaulted ceilings lined with twenty-three-carat gold leaf, and oversized windows. Thirty-six plaster cast statues perched around the balcony level, depicting legionnaires in various poses with eagle-adorned shields, capes, tunics, and helmets.

"It's undergoing repair." Cutty pointed up at some scaffolding. "The ceiling was damaged by an earthquake in 2011."

Built in 1907, Union Station was the Amtrak headquarters and served two commuter rail services and three bus lines.

"Thousands of visitors pass through here every day."

"I could sit here and people watch all afternoon." Jada had previously visited the nation's capital during school field trips. Even though DC was only forty-one miles from Baltimore, it was a whole different world.

After checking in to the Westin Hotel, the couple dined at P.F. Chang's. It was Cutty's first time eating at the popular Chinese restaurant, and Jada had insisted she treat him for his Valentine's gift. They enjoyed some chicken lettuce wraps as an appetizer then shared two dishes and rice for the main course.

They held hands as they walked the two blocks back to their hotel.

Their room had been upgraded to a junior suite. Jada used the larger of the two bathrooms adjoining the bedroom to change. When she emerged, Cutty sat in a chair facing the floor-to-ceiling window overlooking the city lights. He wore comfy plaid pants with a navy tank top.

Upon hearing Jada's soft footsteps, Cutty turned toward her. His eyes widened at the sight of her. She wore a short baby-pink negligee with a matching three-quarter-sleeved nightgown. Jada sat gracefully on Cutty's lap and wrapped her arms around his muscular shoulders.

"You look lovely," Cutty commented. "Is this new?" He softly fingered the silky material of her sleeve.

"It's a gift from my aunty. She gave it to me last night while I was packing for the trip."

"Sweet," Cutty remarked.

The two kissed.

Cutty toyed with Jada's hair. "Are you tired?"

"I feel alive," Jada purred. She kissed him more.

"What's the day without a little night?" Cutty whispered into Jada's ear.

They slowly stood. Cutty took Jada's hand and led her toward the king-size bed.

He turned and faced Jada, his eyes slowly scanning her body. "It's a shame to take off such a pretty nightie."

"It would be a shame not to," Jada responded quickly.

They helped each other undress. Cutty picked Jada up in his arms and lay her carefully on top of the bed. They made love.

The next morning, Jada awoke to the sound of running water. She looked around and realized Cutty was in the shower, getting ready for his conference. After several minutes, Cutty emerged from the main bathroom. He wore new skinny jeans and a white T-shirt.

"You look so handsome," Jada complimented him.

Cutty walked to her side of the bed and sat down. "Happy Valentine's Day, Sweet Pea." He kissed her.

"Happy Valentine's Day to you too, my love," Jada replied.

"Are you ready to be pampered today?"

"Oh yeah," Jada said enthusiastically.

Just then, someone knocked at the door.

"That'll be the room service I ordered," Cutty announced as he headed toward the door. A hotel waiter pushed a cart in and set up the table beside the seating area and television. "How's this, sir?" he asked.

"Excellent," Cutty exclaimed as he signed the room service receipt. He pulled a ten-dollar bill from his back pocket and tipped the gentleman.

"Thank you," Jada called after the waiter wished them a good day and headed out the door.

"I think I put my wallet in the nightstand. Can you please check the drawer beside the bed?" Cutty asked.

"Sure thing." Jada wiggled her way over to Cutty's side of the bed and opened the top drawer of the nightstand but didn't see a wallet inside. Instead, Jada found a light-gray jewelry box with a red bow on top. "Oh, Cutty... what have you done?"

"Why don't you open it and find out?" Cutty suggested.

Jada lifted the Zales jewelry box and opened it. Inside was a two-toned rose-and-white-gold heart-shaped diamond pendant on a white-gold chain. "It's beautiful. I love it!"

"Here, let me help." Cutty walked over to Jada, took the necklace out of the box, and undid the clasp.

Jada turned away from him so he could place the necklace around her neck and do it up.

"There, that looks better," Cutty affirmed.

"Thank you." Jada stood and faced Cutty. "You spoil me. How will I ever repay you?" She kissed his lips.

"Oh, I can think of ways," Cutty replied playfully.

Jada walked into the bathroom to view her new necklace in the mirror. It looked stunning next to her pink nightie. She slipped on her nightgown and followed Cutty toward the breakfast table.

After eating a delightful breakfast of sausage, eggs, hash browns, and freshly squeezed orange juice, Cutty brushed his teeth and put on the olive-green hoodie Jada had given him for Christmas.

Jada walked him to the door, where they hugged and kissed.

"Enjoy the course."

"I'm looking forward to it. Enjoy your spa day. And be ready to dance the night away." Cutty winked before leaving their suite.

Jada smiled to herself. She took another look at her necklace in the mirror. *How did I ever get so lucky?* She pushed the room service cart outside into the hallway for the hotel staff to retrieve.

After a long soak in the bathtub, Jada donned some leggings, a sweatshirt, and flip-flops and took the elevator to the first level.

"Welcome to the spa," the lady at the front desk greeted her. "You must be Jada."

"That's me." Jada loved the aroma. She had read that the spa used essential oils, such as lavender and eucalyptus, to create a relaxing environment.

"I'm Sophia. I'll be doing your manicure and pedicure today. Follow me." The esthetician had a soothing voice.

Jada followed her to an open area down the hall. They stopped at a sink, where Sophia instructed Jada to wash and dry her hands. Afterward, Sophia ushered her to the first of several stations that filled the room. One other guest, an older woman, was being treated several seats away.

"Please take a seat. I'll do your hands first. That way, your fingers will be nice and dry by the time you leave."

"Sounds good." Jada was ready to be pampered.

She'd had manicures at the mall with Chloe, but they'd never set foot in such a lovely salon before. The room was decorated in earth tones with pictures of waterfalls and rainforests on the walls. The soft electronic music playing in the background enhanced the tranquil vibe. *I wish Chloe were here.*

Sophia instructed Jada to place one hand in a manicure soaking bowl. She took Jada's free hand and began shaping her nails with an emery board.

"Do you live in Washington?" Sophia asked.

"No, I'm from Baltimore. My boyfriend is attending a conference at the hotel."

"Ah, will you be doing some sightseeing?"

"Possibly tomorrow, before we head back," Jada replied. "I have school on Monday, and Cutty—that's my boyfriend—has to work. We'll be attending a dinner and dance tonight here at the hotel."

"Do you have a fancy dress to wear?"

"Yes," Jada answered. "It's black and strapless with a sweetheart neckline."

She felt a tickling sensation on the tips of her fingers as Sophia expertly beveled the file downward.

"What color would you like?" Sophia pointed to a row of nail polish.

"How about this one?" Jada singled out a soft-pink bottle.

"Lovely, you'll be the belle of the ball." Sophia began to trim Jada's cuticles.

Cutty returned to the suite just after four in the afternoon.

Jada proudly showed off her freshly manicured fingers and toenails. "How was the conference?"

"Good, the speakers were excellent. The focus was encouraging self-esteem in America's youth." Cutty yawned. It had been a long day.

"Sounds like it was right up your alley."

They lay down on the bed for a short nap.

After a dozing off for an hour, Cutty got up and changed into his dark-gray suit and tie in the smaller bathroom. Jada used the larger en suite to touch up her makeup then slipped on the dress she'd purchased on sale at Macy's. After stepping into the sparkly-silver high-heeled sandals she'd bought at DSW, Jada walked out of the bathroom and over to where Cutty sat watching television.

"Would you mind giving me a hand with my dress?" Jada asked, presenting her back to Cutty.

He zipped the dress and fastened the hook at the top. When she turned around and faced him, Cutty was blown away by her beauty. The heart-shaped diamond pendant sparkled on her collarbone. The necklace paired well with the white-gold hoops he had given her for Christmas.

"Do I look okay?"

"You look perfect," Cutty reassured Jada, giving her a head-to-toe scan with his eyes. He loved her hair.

Jada had curled it in large waves and let it hang down, unpinned.

"Thank you for bringing me here," Jada said sincerely. "You look handsome." She ran her hand along his arm.

"My pleasure," Cutty replied. "I couldn't imagine spending Valentine's Day any other way." He kissed her forehead, inhaling the scent of her perfume. "I guess it's that time," Cutty announced after looking at his iPhone.

Jada took a short, light-gray faux fur jacket off a hanger in the closet and slipped it on. Then she picked up a sparkly-silver clutch purse.

"Stunning" was all Cutty could say.

The pair caught the elevator to the lobby and walked a ways before finding the Aspen Ballroom. After presenting their tickets to the hostess, they were instructed to take their seats at a numbered table.

"I'm Cutty, and this is my girlfriend, Jada." Cutty introduced himself to the three couples seated at their designated table.

Their dinner companions were from neighboring cities, and at least one of each pair worked for the Department of Health and Human Services.

When their table was called, Cutty stood and pulled the chair back for Jada. "After you," he said as they made their way to the buffet.

"Look at all the food," Jada exclaimed.

They began at the salad selection then progressed to the hot food.

Cutty tapped Jada's arm and discreetly pointed to a nearby table. "Save room for dessert." The table was laden with a selection of cakes, squares, and cut fruit. A large chocolate fountain sat in the middle.

"May I have your attention please?" A man at the podium addressed the crowd as they finished eating. He introduced himself and welcomed all the guests, mentioning some of the highlights of the day, then he introduced the guest of honor, who happened to be the honorable Sylvia Burns, secretary of Health and Human Services.

The secretary, who resided in Washington, DC, explained a little about the health department under the federal government. Its goal was protecting the health of all Americans and providing essential services, while its motto was to improve the health, safety, and well-being of America. Sylvia Burns would be presenting one citizen from each of the fifty states who was employed in the Health and Human Services Department with an award in recognition of their outstanding contributions to their community.

Secretary Burns first read aloud the names of the recipients who, due to distance and commitments, were unable to attend the conference. Then she read the names of the recipients who were in attendance. One by one, the recipients made their way to the podium to receive their awards and shake hands with the secretary. "For the state of Maryland, it gives me great pleasure to call on Chad 'Cutty' Jones," Sylvia announced.

Jada turned toward Cutty in astonishment. "Oh my goodness, Cutty."

Cutty blushed and shook his head in disbelief. Then he stood and made his way to the podium. Not only did he shake hands with Sylvia Burns. A picture was taken of them while Cutty held the award.

"Thank you, Madam Secretary," Cutty uttered humbly.

"Congratulations, keep up the excellent work," Sylvia Burns replied.

Smiling, Cutty made his way back to the table.

Jada was quick to stand and give him a hug and kiss on his cheek. "I am so proud of you!"

"Thanks, Sweet Pea," Cutty said bashfully.

Their dinner companions rose to shake Cutty's hand. Afterward, they took their seats and listened as the madam secretary called out names and states of the remaining recipients.

"I wasn't expecting this," Cutty whispered to Jada.

"No doubt," Jada replied. "But you deserve it. Think of all the effort you put into the boxing gym and improving the quality of life for those boys."

"Thanks. I'm certain my supervisor, Linda, had something to do with nominating me," Cutty furthered. "I'm going to send her a quick text." Cutty pulled out his iPhone and typed.

"Good idea," Jada agreed, turning to the couple beside her and smiling.

Before long, the host announced that the award ceremony was over and that the dance would start shortly. The audience gave one final round of applause. Jada excused herself and headed to the nearest washroom. Cutty did the same. When they met back up inside the ballroom, the lights were dimmed, and a disc jockey had begun playing music.

"Did you hear back from your supervisor?" Jada inquired.

"Oh, yeah," Cutty informed. "Linda congratulated me and said to enjoy our evening. And that we'll talk when I get back to work on Monday." Cutty chuckled.

"It's been such an exciting weekend," Jada acknowledged. "I can't wait to share the news with everyone."

Cutty stood facing Jada, his arms encircling her. A trending dance beat came over the speakers.

"Would you like to dance?" he asked.

"I'd love to." Jada took Cutty's hand and led him toward the center of the dance floor. They enjoyed several dances together and took breaks for water. Some fairly good dancers were in attendance, but Jada was definitely exceptional. And she brought out the confidence in Cutty, making him a sharp dancing partner.

Chapter Eighteen

IT WAS SUNDAY MORNING, JULY 17, 2016, almost two years to the date since Jada and Cutty had gone on their first picnic at the Maryland Zoo. Not only was Jada anxiously awaiting Cutty's arrival at her aunt's town house. She couldn't wait to surprise him with the dessert she had made for their anniversary outing.

She took one last look at herself in the hall mirror. She wore baby-pink shorts and a white tank top with appliqué flowers on the front. She chose to wear her white tennis shoes and socks from her cheer outfit. She hadn't tried out for the cheerleading squad her second year of college.

Instead, she'd taken training for beginner's hatha yoga and was teaching it two evenings a week at the boxing gym. Mostly young teenage girls attended Jada's class, and some of them even used the gym equipment, which meant gym memberships were increasing.

When the doorbell rang, Jada was quick to answer it. She greeted Cutty with a kiss on the lips.

"Are you ready, Sweet Pea?" He wore denim shorts and a gray Baltimore Orioles tank top with their orange-and-black logo.

"Oh yeah. I'm excited to see the animals. It's been a whole year," Jada informed him enthusiastically.

She followed Cutty outside onto the landing and locked the door. Then the pair headed to the bus stop. They didn't have to wait too long. After transferring to another bus, they arrived at their destination around ten o'clock. Cutty insisted on buying Jada's ticket, since she had prepared their picnic lunch. They leisurely strolled the zoo exhibits and, as usual, began with the African Journey.

"Wouldn't it be fun to go to Africa someday and see the animals in their natural habitats?" Jada asked.

"That would be cool," Cutty agreed. "It would be a long flight, though."

They spent a good twenty minutes at the Penguin Coast Exhibit, where the couple watched the zoo workers feed the penguins fish. Jada never tired of the ritual. When they arrived at the giraffe enclosure, Jada bought an acacia branch so Cutty could feed the young animal. It had become their tradition. It always put a big smile on Cutty's face to interact with the lovely creatures.

After completing the African Journey, the couple made their way past the food court.

"How is this spot?" Jada pointed to an empty picnic table.

But Cutty had his eye on a more secluded spot. "Actually, how about we take that table?" He motioned to one a little farther away. "It has more shade."

"Sure thing," Jada replied, and the pair made their way over to the vacant spot. Jada began unpacking her backpack.

"What did you make for us, Sweet Pea?" Cutty asked hungrily.

"I made egg-salad sandwiches on Alpine bread. And I have some sliced vegetables with ranch dressing for dipping."

"Sounds divine," Cutty exclaimed. He opened a water bottle and took a sip.

"Just make sure you save some room for dessert," Jada suggested with a grin.

"Oh, and what might that be?" Cutty inquired.

"It's a surprise," Jada said. "But I'm fairly certain you'll like it."

Cutty smiled. "I always enjoy what you and your aunt Ruby prepare for me. I feel pretty blessed to have you in my life, always pampering me. You and all the guys are my tribe. Life is good as far as I'm concerned."

And it was about to get even better.

Lunch was tasty, but Cutty only ate one sandwich, seemingly so he would have room for Jada's dessert.

"I like the veggies and dip," he complimented Jada.

"That's good. We need three to five servings of vegetables per day," Jada responded.

"And how many servings of fruit do we need?" Cutty inquired.

"Two to four servings per day," Jada replied.

She pulled out a plastic food-storage container and opened the lid. Inside were four homemade bars. She passed the container to Cutty, and he carefully took one out.

"What have we here?" Cutty asked.

"Blueberry oat bars," Jada answered.

"Nice." Cutty beamed. "You know how much I love blueberries!" He chuckled and took a bite. "Superb," he complimented, chewing. He gave her a thumbs-up.

Jada was pleased. She enjoyed trying new recipes, especially ones Cutty would like. "The oatmeal counts as a whole grain, and we need three to five servings of them per day." Not only was Jada interested in nutrition for herself. She discussed it with the young girls in her yoga class. Like Cutty, she believed fitness and nutrition went hand in hand.

"Can I have more?" Cutty asked.

"Absolutely," Jada replied. "I have a whole pan of them back home. You can take some to your suite later if you'd like." Her little surprise was a hit, which gave her confidence. She loved seeing Cutty happy.

"Did you know July is national blueberry month?"

"No, I didn't know that," Jada responded.

"The United States Department of Agriculture proclaimed it back in 2003," Cutty furthered. "Highbush blueberries are harvested from mid-April until early October, but the harvest reaches its peak in July."

"That makes sense." Jada pondered the information. After Jada finished eating a blueberry oatmeal bar, she tidied up the lunch stuff and zipped her backpack.

"Shall we sit in the shade for a little while?" Cutty suggested.

"If you like." Jada followed Cutty over to the large tree that provided shade for their table.

Cutty sat down first and opened his arms, inviting Jada to sit near him. Jada sat down, and Cutty embraced her.

"It's such a beautiful day," Cutty commented.

"Indeed. We always have nice weather for the zoo," Jada agreed.

"Have I told you lately how much I love you?" Cutty asked.

"Aw. I think so. But I never grow tired of hearing you say it," Jada replied. "I love you too." The heat made her a little drowsy. She could almost take a nap.

She was about to ask Cutty if she could lie on his lap when he spoke.

"I need to ask you something." Cutty sounded serious. He pulled away from their embrace and fidgeted a little. Then he knelt on a knee and brought his right hand out from his side. In it was a square box. He opened the lid to reveal a brilliant round-diamond engagement ring set in a white-gold band. "Will you marry me, Jada?"

"Oh my goodness, Cutty!" Jada was shocked but in a good way. She looked from the ring into Cutty's eyes then back at the ring again. It was gorgeous. In fact, she had never seen a diamond ring so large before. She trembled with nervous energy and placed her left hand over her mouth. "Ohhh," she said again.

"What do you think?" Cutty asked.

After she caught her breath, Jada managed to get her words out. "I think that it is the most exquisite thing I have ever seen."

He carefully pulled the ring out of its box and took Jada's left hand away from her mouth. Then, he slowly placed the ring on her fourth finger. It fit nicely, though Jada's hand was still trembling. "I'll take that as a yes?"

"Yes. Oh, Cutty, yes!"

Jada threw herself into Cutty's arms, and the couple shared a romantic kiss. Afterward, they smiled at one another. Jada held out her left hand, and they were both bedazzled by the sheer beauty of the ring next to her skin.

"Does anyone else know?" Jada asked.

"No, only you," Cutty replied, smiling lovingly at Jada.

"I can't wait to show Aunt Ruby and Chloe." Jada moved her hand around a little, glancing at her ring from different angles. It was mesmerizing. "When should we get married?"

"I was thinking two summers from now," Cutty answered. "Once you finish your undergraduate degree. How does that sound?"

"It sounds perfect. Right before I begin law school." Jada looked pleased. "May we have a June wedding?"

"Certainly. We'll have to book Rev Joe and St. Peter's Church," Cutty added.

"I can't wait to start planning it," Jada exclaimed.

The couple had attended Elias and Samantha's wedding the summer before. It had been a decent size, and Cutty had looked very handsome as the best man. Jada remembered Samantha talking about all the small details that went into pulling off such a marvelous feat.

"It'll be so exciting to shop for the wedding dress," Jada announced. She was over-the-moon thrilled. "Oh, and we must have a dance at the wedding."

"Most definitely," Cutty agreed. He couldn't imagine a wedding without one, especially when it involved Jada. He was happy she'd accepted his marriage proposal. Word would spread soon enough about their engagement. He breathed a sigh of relief.

Jada no longer felt tired. In fact, she was energized like never before. "Cutty?"

"Yes," he replied.

"Can we take a ride on the zoo train, in honor of my uncle Roy?" Jada requested. "I feel like celebrating."

"Let's do it," Cutty approved.

The newly engaged couple walked over to the ticket booth and bought two tickets for the train. They didn't have to wait too long until it departed.

"All aboard!" the conductor called out.

"Yes!" everyone yelled, including Jada and Cutty.

Chapter Nineteen

THE BIG DAY FINALLY ARRIVED. It had been almost two years since Cutty proposed to Jada at the Maryland Zoo. Jada had recently completed her bachelor's degree in commerce and had been accepted into law school effective the beginning of September.

It was Saturday, June 9, and Jada was calmer than she'd expected to be. Everything they had planned was falling into place. But to Jada and Cutty's credit, they had kept things fairly simple. They wanted a day to remember and cherish, not one fraught with stress. Their goal was to enjoy this occasion with their family and friends.

Jada curled her tresses then swept her hair to the right side, letting it fall down her back and shoulders. Her makeup consisted of eye shadow, eyeliner, mascara, blush, and lip gloss. Simple yet classy.

Stepping into her mermaid dress brought back memories of shopping with her aunt Ruby and Chloe the previous summer. It was the third dress Jada had tried on, and she knew in a heartbeat that it was the one. The strapless tulle gown had a hand-beaded sweetheart neckline and an embroidered and hand-patterned beaded dropped waist. The bodice featured floral appliqué with an illusion V-back trimmed with crystal buttons that cascaded down to a softly ruffled hemline and chapel-length train.

When she put on her shoes, she felt like Cinderella. They were the sparkly-silver high-heeled sandals she'd bought to accent her black dress on her first Valentine's Day with Cutty, in Washington, DC. The shoes were her "something old" while her wedding dress was the "something new" in keeping with the tradition of the old English rhyme. Jada, being the scholar she was, had read that something old represented continuity, while something new offered optimism for the future.

Next, she put on the white-gold pearl drop earrings Aunt Ruby had lent her. They had been a gift from Uncle Roy to his wife on their fifteenth wedding anniversary. The "something borrowed" symbolized borrowed happiness. It was fitting, as their time with Roy had been limited. Jada felt honored to be wearing the earrings.

Last but not least, she slipped the blue garter belt Cutty had purchased for her onto her left leg, placing it above her knee. It was the perfect spot, as her mermaid dress flared out right above her knees, so the close-fitting band didn't stand out under her dress. The "something blue" stood for purity, love, and fidelity.

Jada took a look at herself in the full-length mirror hanging on the back of her bedroom door, pleased with what she saw. She closed her eyes and said a silent prayer. *Thank you, God, for Cutty. Please give him courage as he prepares for our special day. Amen.*

Suddenly, she heard voices in the hallway. Chloe, her maid of honor, was using Brodie's room to get ready. Aunt Ruby had slipped out earlier to have her hair done with her stylist. *She must be back.* Jada opened her bedroom door and stepped into the hallway.

Aunt Ruby stopped talking midsentence. "Oh, sweetie!" she exclaimed. Her face broke into a smile as she placed her right hand above her heart.

"Jada, you look stunning!" Chloe wore a full-length soft-pink mermaid gown. It was strapless with a sweetheart neckline as well. Her curly hair fell just below her shoulders, and the sides were pinned up.

"Thank you both. Chloe, you look beautiful." Jada couldn't be prouder of her friend, who had recently completed her bachelor's degree in nursing and was working at Saint Agnes Hospital in the labor and delivery unit.

"If you two are okay for the moment, I'll just slip into my room and put on my dress," Ruby announced.

"Yeah. We are all good, Aunty," Jada replied.

Ruby walked past the girls and entered her bedroom.

"I was hoping to have a moment alone with you," Jada said to Chloe. She beckoned her friend to enter her bedroom with her. From inside her top dresser drawer, Jada pulled out a square jewelry box and handed it to Chloe.

"What's this for?" Chloe asked.

"It's just a little something for being my maid of honor," Jada replied happily. "Open it."

Chloe removed the pink ribbon from the box and lifted the lid. Inside was a white-gold necklace with a single pearl. The pearl was attached to the chain via a white-gold infinity loop that featured tiny diamonds. "Oh, Jada, this is so lovely!" she exclaimed as she held it up.

"We will be friends for eternity," Jada proclaimed. "May I put that on for you?"

Chloe handed her the necklace, and Jada carefully undid the clasp. After placing it on her neck, Jada turned with Chloe and looked into the dresser mirror.

"It looks perfect with your dress."

"Aw. Thank you so much," Chloe said. "I am honored to be in your bridal party."

The two friends shared a hug.

"Before long, you'll be standing up with me," Chloe added.

Brodie had proposed to Chloe the previous summer, and the couple had planned their wedding for August. That gave Jada and Cutty time to settle into their town house after their honeymoon. For their wedding gifts, Ruby had generously given each couple a down payment to buy their first homes. She had been saving the money since receiving the life insurance from Roy's passing.

"I can't wait for your wedding," Jada responded enthusiastically. "Soon, we'll be family."

Just then, Ruby entered the room, wearing a three-quarter-length mauve-colored dress with silver sandals.

"Look at you, Aunty!" Jada exclaimed.

"Oh yeah. Rev Joe won't be able to keep his eyes off you, Ruby," Chloe added.

The reverend and Ruby had been dating for a few months. It was inevitable, given the fact that the pair spent so much time together and Ruby enjoyed cooking for the reverend.

Ruby chuckled. "We cleaned up nicely."

They heard the front door close on the main level.

"That'll be Brodie," Ruby said. "He just stepped out to pick up the flowers."

"Is it safe to come upstairs?" Brodie called.

"Yes, come up," his mom replied.

Brodie bounded up the stairs. He wore a dark-gray suit. "Woo-eee!" he exclaimed as he saw the ladies. "My three girls look gorgeous." He gave them each a kiss. Brodie was a journeyman electrician and worked full-time at Coleman's Plumbing and Electrical.

"You're looking pretty snazzy yourself," Jada replied. "Thank you for getting the flowers."

"No problem. I dropped the boutonnieres off at the church. Rev Joe will give them to the guys."

"We should probably head there now," Chloe announced. "Jada, do you have everything?"

"I just have to grab my bag," Jada answered.

Ruby shut off the lights, and the four of them walked down the stairs. Brodie opened a large cardboard box sitting on the coffee table. He passed out the two bouquets to Jada and Chloe and helped his mom put on her wristlet corsage. Then Chloe pinned Brodie's boutonniere onto his lapel. The bouquets both contained yellow and a variety of pink peonies held together by white lace, while the boutonnieres contained white peonies.

"I almost forgot," Brodie announced. "I need to snap a few pictures of you ladies."

"Oh, goodness," Ruby replied. "It totally slipped my mind."

The three ladies stood by the wing chair, and Brodie began taking pictures. He had purchased the camera to be used at both weddings and honeymoons. After Jada was satisfied with the results, she took some pictures of Chloe and Brodie together as well as Ruby and Brodie.

"We need some pictures of the cousins," Chloe ordered. She took the camera and snapped some pictures of Jada and Brodie. "There, I think that's all the combinations for now." She handed the camera back to Brodie.

"Are we good to go?" Brodie inquired.

The ceremony was scheduled for two in the afternoon.

"Yeah. Let's go!" Jada exclaimed. She started to get butterflies in her tummy. She couldn't wait to be Cutty's wife.

Elias drove his wife, Cutty, and Levi to St. Peter's Church at one thirty.

The reverend met the group at the church entrance. "What a fine-looking bunch you young people make," he noted.

"Thank you, Reverend," Cutty replied.

He and his best man, Levi, wore dark-gray suits. Dressed in a bright-blue suit, Elias was the usher. Samantha wore a lovely butter-yellow sundress with gold wedge-heeled shoes.

"Here are your boutonnieres." The reverend handed them to the guys.

Samantha helped Elias place his, while Cutty and Levi helped one another with the task of pinning the flowers to their lapels.

"Cutty, may I have a few words with you?" Rev Joe asked.

"Absolutely." Cutty followed him into the rectory.

"How are you holding up today?" the reverend inquired.

"I've never felt better," Cutty stated confidently.

"I'm glad to hear that," the reverend said. "I just wanted a couple of minutes alone with you to say a few words of prayer."

"That would be awesome," Cutty said.

"This is a pretty big step you and Jada are taking today, and I just want to wish you both all the best that married life has to offer," Rev Joe proclaimed. "And I also want to let you know that I am here for you, Cutty, if you ever need to talk."

"Thank you, Reverend. I appreciate that." Cutty smiled.

The reverend was like a father to him. It gave Cutty great comfort to know he could reach out to Rev Joe if ever the occasion arose, especially since his parents lived in North Carolina.

The reverend took ahold of Cutty's left arm, and both men bowed their heads.

"Heavenly Father, we are so blessed to be in Your presence on this beautiful day. I ask You, Father, to bless our brother Cutty as he prepares to take Jada as his lovely wife. Please give him wisdom and guidance to shoulder any troubles that may arise. Most of all, Father, bless their union so it may be fruitful and filled with joy and happiness. I ask these things in Your name, Dear Father. In Jesus's name, we pray. Amen."

"Amen," Cutty added. "Thank you."

The two men hugged.

"Well, I guess it's about that time." The reverend looked at his watch. It was 1:50 p.m.

The two men walked into the sanctuary. Cutty followed Rev Joe toward the altar and took his place beside Levi. The reverend adjusted his bible and notes.

Cutty looked up to see his parents being guided to their seats by Elias. Marvin and Delores Jones had driven up from Sneads Ferry three days prior and were staying with friends. Cutty smiled and nodded at them. His mom blew him a kiss. She wore a light-blue dress, while his dad looked sharp in his navy suit.

He wondered how Jada was doing. The bride had so much more preparation to attend to than the groom. *Knowing Jada, she'll ace this.*

The church pianist began playing a hymn as a few more guests arrived. It wasn't a big wedding, as the couple didn't have large families or a big group of friends.

Samantha appeared in the doorway and gave Cutty a thumbs-up to let him know the bridal party had arrived and were ready to make their entrance. Cutty then nodded to the reverend, and he, in turn, alerted the pianist. Brodie made his way to the front of the church and took a seat in a pew. He smiled at Cutty.

Once she finished the hymn, the pianist began playing "Canon in D" by Johann Pachelbel, the popular wedding song written around 1680. The reverend asked the audience to stand for the bride, and the guests stood. Chloe walked in first, slowly and smiling as she carried her bouquet in both hands. Once at the front of the church, Chloe took her position to the left of the altar and turned slightly so she had a good view of the bride's entrance.

Ruby walked her niece slowly down the aisle. Jada looked radiant as she gracefully walked the fifty feet to the altar. Her eyes sought Cutty's, and when she found them, he rewarded her with a look of adoration. Cutty and Levi had chosen the perfect hue of gray to wear. The boutonnieres looked elegant on their lapels.

Once they reached the altar, Ruby hugged her niece before handing her over to Cutty.

"You look amazing," Cutty whispered to his bride-to-be.

Jada smiled in return and whispered, "Thanks. So do you."

She stood to the left of Cutty, in keeping with the tradition that stemmed from the old days of marriage by capture. The groom needed to keep his right hand—or fighting hand, which held a sword—free in case he needed to defend his bride from any suitors who might try to steal her away at the last minute. Also, since the heart was located on one's left, the bride stood under the groom's heart.

The reverend asked, "Who gives this woman to be married to this man?"

"I do," Ruby replied.

"You may be seated." The reverend addressed Ruby and the guests.

Everyone except the wedding party and Rev Joe sat down.

The reverend began with his greeting. "The grace of our Lord Jesus Christ, the love of God, and the communion of the Holy Spirit be with you all."

"And also with you," the guests replied in unison.

"Dear friends," the reverend continued. "We have come together in the presence of God to witness the marriage of Jada and Chad, to surround them in our prayers, and to share in their joy.

"The scriptures teach us that the bond and covenant of marriage is a gift of God, a holy mystery in which two become one flesh, an image of the union of Christ and the church. As Jada and Chad give themselves to each other today, we remember that at Cana in Galilee, our Lord Jesus Christ made the wedding feast a sign of God's reign of love.

"Let us enter into this celebration confident that, through the Holy Spirit, Christ is present with us now also. We pray that this couple may fulfill God's purpose for the whole of their lives."

The reverend addressed Cutty first in the declaration of intention. "Chad, will you have Jada to be your wife, to live together in the covenant of marriage? Will you love her, comfort her, honor and keep her, in sickness and in health, and forsaking all others, be faithful to her as long as you both shall live?"

"I will," Cutty responded.

The reverend addressed Jada. "Jada, will you have Chad to be your husband, to live together in the covenant of marriage? Will you love him, comfort him, honor and keep him, in sickness and health, and forsaking all others, be faithful to him as long as you both shall live?"

"I will," Jada responded. By God's grace, she didn't cry, though she trembled slightly.

Sensing that, Cutty gently squeezed her hand and winked at her.

The reverend addressed the guests. "Will you, the families of Jada and Chad, give your love and blessing to this new family?"

"We will," the families answered.

"Will all of you, by God's grace, do everything in your power to uphold and care for these two persons in their life together?"

"We will," the guests answered.

Everyone bowed their heads as Rev Joe announced, "Let us pray. Eternal God, our creator and redeemer, as You gladdened the wedding at Cana in Galilee by the presence of Your Son, so bring Your joy to this wedding by His presence now. Look in favor upon Chad and Jada, and grant that they, rejoicing in all your gifts, may at length celebrate the unending marriage feast with Christ our Lord, who lives and reigns with You and the Holy Spirit, one God, now and forever."

"Amen," the guests replied.

The reverend proceeded to share three scripture readings: two psalms from the Old Testament followed by one from the gospels. Following his short sermon, the guests all sang one hymn accompanied by the pianist. A period of silence for reflection came after the song.

The reverend instructed Cutty and Jada to hold hands. Levi passed two rings to Rev Joe, who then placed them atop his bible and held them in front of the couple.

"I take you, Jada, to be my wife from this day forward, to join with you and share all that is to come, and I promise to be faithful to you until death parts us." Cutty selected the diamond eternity wedding band and slid it onto Jada's left ring finger. It sparkled brilliantly.

"I take you, Chad, to be my husband from this day forward, to join with you and share all that is to come, and I promise to be faithful to you until death parts us." Jada selected the remaining masculine white-gold wedding band, which contained the slightest accent of rose gold, and slid it onto Cutty's left ring finger.

The reverend spoke. "Bless these rings, O God. May those who wear them live in love and fidelity and continue in Your service all the days of their lives, through Jesus Christ our Lord. Amen."

"Chad and Jada, by their promises before God and in the presence of this assembly, have joined themselves to one another as husband and wife. Those whom God has joined together let no one separate." The reverend placed his hand above the couple's heads and said a marriage blessing, followed by prayers of intercession for the world.

After reciting the Lord's Prayer with his guests, the reverend spoke. "The peace of Christ be with you always."

The guests replied, "And with you also."

Finally, Cutty was able to kiss his bride. Their kiss was deep and held promise as Cutty cupped the back of Jada's head.

"The blessed and Holy Trinity make you strong in faith and love, defend you on every side, and guide you in truth and peace, now and forever." The reverend proclaimed God's blessing.

"Amen," replied the guests.

"Go in peace. Serve the Lord" were the reverend's final words.

"Thanks be to God," the guests replied.

Cutty and Jada walked off to the side to sign their marriage documents. Chloe and Levi followed and bore witness by adding their names to the legal papers. Samantha took pictures of the sacred act. Once finished, Cutty and Jada walked back toward the altar.

The reverend announced, "I would like to introduce you to Mr. and Mrs. Chad Jones."

The guests clapped and stood as the beaming couple walked down the aisle and into the church entrance. They formed a receiving line alongside Chloe and Levi. Just then, the church bells began to ring. It was a lovely sound.

Michael and his parents were the first to hug the wedding party and wished the newlyweds much love and happiness as they made their way to leave. Cutty's parents were next in line. After congratulating the couple, Marvin and Delores hugged Ruby and Brodie, as they were family.

Olivia, Jada's friend from college, greeted the couple. Beside her was her boyfriend, a tall, handsome basketball player from the same school. Then Linda, Cutty's supervisor, along with her husband congratulated the pair. Once the guests had finished greeting the wedding party, Rev Joe congratulated the couple and told them how well they had done for the ceremony.

"Jada and I can't thank you enough, Reverend, for all you've done for us," Cutty offered.

"Yes. It was such a beautiful service," Jada added.

"Well, you two make it fairly easy for an old minister such as myself to deliver a precious rite," the reverend said.

Brodie approached the couple. "Are you two ready to head off for the photo shoot?"

"You bet," Cutty replied.

"I'll see you all at supper," the reverend said as he stepped away.

"Sounds good, Reverend," Jada answered.

"Mom packed some snacks in the cooler for y'all," Brodie announced.

"Thank goodness," Jada exclaimed, "because I'm hungry."

"No doubt, cuz." Brodie chuckled.

He summoned his mom, who was talking to her cousin Sally. The group made their way outside into the parking lot and climbed into the church Suburban. After helping themselves to some snacks, Cutty, Jada, and Samantha sat in Elias's BMW sedan. The two vehicles headed toward a lovely park near the Inner Harbor, where wedding photos would be taken. On the back of the BMW, Elias had placed a Just Married sign. It was from his and Samantha's wedding three years prior.

The wedding supper took place in the church basement and was prepared by the women of St. Peter's parish. The soul-food feast consisted of fried chicken, collard greens with ham hocks, macaroni and cheese, green beans, candied yams, and corn bread.

Brodie did a fine job of being the master of ceremonies. He didn't suffer from stage fright one bit. Chloe and Levi each gave beautiful tributes to their friends, the newlyweds.

Then, it was Cutty's turn to say a few words. "Friends, family, and Reverend Joe, Jada and I can't thank you all enough for celebrating this special day with us. All of your hard work has paid off, as we are now able to relax after enjoying such an amazing meal prepared by the women of St. Peter's."

He raised his glass of wine, and the guests followed suit in toasting the church women.

"Before we begin the dance, I want to thank Ruby for the lovely cake she created for our wedding. We will enjoy it a bit later." Cutty motioned to a table off to the side that was adorned with a beautiful naked three-tiered blueberry lemon cake topped with blueberries, raspberries, strawberries, and green foliage. "Ruby knows how much I love blueberries," Cutty added, chuckling. "Thank you, Levi and Chloe, for standing up for us today and for your kind words. It means a lot to Jada and me. Thanks to Brodie and Samantha for taking pictures of the wedding. I'm sure those will turn out amazing. Thanks to Elias for being my personal chauffeur. It's not every day I get to ride around in a polished BMW sedan."

Everyone laughed at that.

"I'd like to thank my parents for traveling from Sneads Ferry to support me as I take this next step in the journey of life. Without your love and determination, I would not have made it to this place. I am forever grateful to you both." Cutty toasted Marvin and Delores. "Love you."

"And now I'd like to propose a toast to my beautiful bride." Cutty faced Jada. "Almost four years ago, you took me to the Maryland Zoo, a little date to cheer me up, and I was captivated by your enthusiasm and love of animals. Not only are you one of the most intelligent and sensitive women I have ever met, you are the most beautiful. I thank God every day for your love and devotion, and I can't wait to see what the future has in store for us. I love you with all my heart and soul." Cutty looked into Jada's eyes as she teared up. "To my gorgeous bride, Jada," Cutty announced, raising his glass.

"To Jada," the guests toasted then clinked their glasses with their spoons.

Cutty obliged them by giving Jada a lingering kiss.

"I love you so much." Jada hugged her husband.

"Mmmm." Cutty sighed. "I meant every word, Sweet Pea." He tenderly embraced his wife.

The guests took the opportunity to freshen up after their delicious supper. D'andre and Tyrell were the dee-jays for the night, and they'd prepared the portable Bose sound system with Bluetooth the night before.

After testing the sound one final time, D'andre gave Cutty the all-clear. The groom took Jada's hand and headed to the dance floor as "That's the Way of the World" by Earth, Wind & Fire began. It was a beautiful rhythm and blues song written in 1975, but the message was timeless. The couple looked stunning as Cutty whisked a graceful Jada around the dance floor in a well-rehearsed modern waltz.

Rev Joe placed his hand on Ruby's shoulder as they watched. "What a beautiful couple," he proclaimed.

"Indeed," Ruby agreed. "Think of the gorgeous babies they will make someday."

The second song the newlyweds had chosen was "September," also by the same band. Chloe and Levi joined the couple on the dance floor. Brodie approached his mom and swept her away from the reverend to dance. Soon, other couples joined in.

During the first break of the dance, Jada and Cutty cut their wedding cake and had fun helping each other take the first bite. The guests enjoyed the delicious dessert along with coffee and tea. Brodie praised Tyrell and D'andre on the fine job of managing the tunes.

"We can't take all the credit," D'andre explained. "Cutty and Jada selected the playlist."

"Yeah, and it's well-ordered," Tyrell agreed.

He and D'andre took turns dancing with their girl-friends to some hip-hop music.

Levi caught the blue garter belt when Cutty tossed it.

Jada was happy for their friend. "It's a sign," she whispered to Cutty.

And when Jada threw her bouquet, it was none other than Olivia who caught it. Not too many single people filled the group, so the chances of success were high. Her boyfriend, being the gentleman he was, escorted Olivia to the dance floor once the music started again. It was a slow song.

"Oh my," Jada exclaimed, referring to Olivia and her escort, as Cutty led her outside for a breath of fresh air.

"You never know." Cutty grinned at Jada.

They planned to spend their first two nights as new-lyweds in their town house not too far from the gym. On Monday morning, the couple was flying to South Africa to go on a safari at Kruger National Park. Cutty had been planning and saving for the honeymoon for two years. Jada was so excited. It was a dream come true.

Cutty stood behind Jada and wrapped her in his arms. He had removed his suit jacket quite some time ago, as it was a warm evening.

"It's been such a beautiful day," Jada said. "Everything went so smoothly."

"It sure did, Sweet Pea." Cutty kissed the side of her head. "I feel so blessed with how life has turned out. I often wonder how I ever got so lucky."

"Well," Jada added, "as my uncle Roy used to say, 'You just have to bloom where you are planted.'" With that, she turned and kissed her husband.

Epilogue

"PUSH, PUSH, PUSH, PUSH, PUSH, push," Suzanne, the labor and delivery nurse, coached Jada.

Finally, a little rest, then Jada felt the next contraction. She tucked her chin toward her chest, took a deep breath, and bore down with all her might, making a deep guttural noise as she did.

"That's it, Jada. That's my girl," Cutty praised. He wiped Jada's forehead with a moist towel.

Another short rest followed by another contraction and a push. Jada was exhausted, but like everywhere else in her life, she wasn't giving up. It was late morning, Friday, May 6, 2022.

Having completed her law degree the previous year and passed the Maryland Bar Exam, Jada had been working full-time as a real estate lawyer in a large law firm. She and Cutty had decided to start a family. They just hadn't expected it to happen so quickly.

"Push, push, push," Suzanne urged.

The baby slid out.

"We have a boy," exclaimed Dr. Hermary, the ob-gyn. "The time is 10:49." She cut the umbilical cord and passed the baby to a waiting pediatrician and his nurse to check the baby's lungs. She concentrated on massaging Jada's abdomen. "Baby number two is head down. This is great news."

Because Jada was having twins two weeks prematurely, she had been given an epidural and was delivering in an operating room at Saint Agnes Hospital. Cutty was dressed in a cap, gown, mask, and face shield like the rest of the neonatal team. He tried to look at his son but focused his attention on Jada. Anything could happen—a drop in the fetal heart rate or a cord wrapped around baby number two's head, which would lead to an emergency caesarean section.

He kissed Jada's forehead. "He looks perfect, Jada. He's in good hands."

Jada smiled at her husband and could see the mixture of excitement and concern in his eyes. She rested some and managed a small sip of water.

After about ten minutes, Dr. Hermary announced, "Your contractions have begun again." She observed the computer screen attached to an electronic fetal monitor.

It didn't take too long for baby number two's head to crown. When it was time, Suzanne told Jada to push, just like she had with the first baby.

Jada tucked her chin toward her chest and pushed. She rested in between and relied on Suzanne to coach her. Cutty did his best to support his wife, wiping her forehead and encouraging her.

Soon, baby number two was delivered.

"It's a girl," Dr. Hermary proclaimed. "The time is 11:28." For the second time, the doctor cut the umbilical cord and passed the newborn to a second pediatrician and his nurse.

"Well done, Sweet Pea." Cutty attended to his wife.

Dr. Hermary delivered the placenta and placed a few sutures. Not too bad, as the babies' weights were four pounds, six ounces and four pounds, four ounces, respectively. "It was a near-textbook delivery." The doctor sounded pleased for the couple.

A nurse popped her head into the delivery room and invited Cutty to come and see the babies in the neonatal intensive care unit. So far, the babies were doing well, she explained to him. They just needed to be under observation as a precaution.

Meanwhile, the anesthesiologist removed the epidural catheter from Jada's back. He advised Jada that she would be able to wiggle her toes and feel sensations in her legs within a couple of hours. Jada thanked him.

Once Dr. Hermary finished her procedures, she sat on the bed beside Jada. "Congratulations, Jada. You did so well!" The doctor gave Jada a gentle hug.

"Thank you, Dr. Hermary," Jada responded, beginning to get a little energy back. Jada loved her ob-gyn. She had so much faith in the experienced middle-aged doctor.

"You'll be taken back to the maternity ward soon, where you'll receive a meal tray," Dr. Hermary instructed. "Try to eat a small amount. See how your tummy responds."

"Oh, that is music to my ears," Jada replied.

A short while later, Cutty returned to the operating room just as Jada was wheeled out.

"How are our babies?" Jada inquired.

"They are so tiny and adorable," Cutty explained. "I didn't get to hold them, but I was able to touch them with gloves on while they lay beside one another in the incubator. They are hooked up to monitors, but the nurses assured me they're stable." Cutty smiled.

"Aw, I can't wait to see them. It shouldn't be too long," Jada told her husband. "I'm headed to the maternity ward now, to recover. Then I'll be fed."

"All right. I should give Ruby an update. Are we sticking with the names?"

"If you are okay with them, Cutty, then I am," Jada replied confidently.

"Absolutely." Cutty leaned over and kissed his wife. "Enjoy your lunch. I'll see you soon, and we'll arrange for you to meet our babies."

Cutty beamed as he walked through the waiting room door.

Ruby looked up from her magazine and gave a slight gasp under her mask. She and her husband, Rev Joe, both stood.

"Have they arrived?" Ruby asked, searching Cutty's eyes.

"Indeed, they have," Cutty shared. "They are together in the NICU. Both are healthy but being monitored as a precaution."

"Fantastic." The reverend shook Cutty's hand.

"And their names?" Ruby questioned. She had been busy all winter making pink and blue quilts. Since marrying Rev Joe the previous summer, Ruby had retired from her job as a school secretary. That had given her more time to volunteer at St. Peter's Church. Soon, her days would be busy helping Jada and Cutty with their twin babies.

"Bryce Roy and Maren Dawn," Cutty answered.

The middle names were after Jada's uncle and mother, who had both passed away some time ago.

"Oh, lovely," Ruby exclaimed as she hugged Cutty. "How's Jada?"

"She's tired but happy. They just moved her into the maternity ward so the epidural can wear off, then she'll be able to spend some time with our babies," Cutty explained. "She's having lunch now."

"Aw, my little sweetie. Did it go okay for her?" Ruby asked, concerned for her niece.

"Jada did amazing. You'd have been so proud of her," Cutty shared.

"I can't tell you how relieved and happy I am right now," Ruby added. "I'll bet you were a supportive partner in the delivery room."

"I tried," Cutty replied. "It was pretty special witnessing the births. The doctors and nurses were awesome."

"Saint Agnes Hospital has an excellent reputation," Ruby stated. "I'll just text Brodie and Chloe the news. Then Joe and I'll go up and visit Jada. Maybe we'll get to peek at the wee babes."

"For sure," Cutty responded. "I'll call my parents, then I'll join you."

The reverend listened to the exchange patiently before adding, "Two healthy babies… two peas in a pod. God has answered our prayers."

Acknowledgements

I AM GRATEFUL FOR THE LOVE and support of my husband, Brent, and our children, Michael and Olivia. You listened to and encouraged me every step of the way as I shared my dream and wrote a story.

Thank you to Carlen, who put me in touch with Jennifer. This is where my journey of self-publishing began. I will forever be indebted to you both.

Thank you to my family, friends, and coworkers—Joan, Kathleen, Kyla, Ann, Sandra, and Tiana—who cheered me on.

Thank you to Lynn, Angie, Amanda, Rashida, and Libybet at Red Adept Editing for your professional services.

Thank you to Streetlight Graphics for the lovely book cover design.

Thank you to webovisko.com for designing my website lorilupul.com

Photo Credit: Wild Earth Photography

Lori was born in North Vancouver and raised on a ranch near Princeton, British Columbia. She has a bachelor's degree in science with a specialization in dental hygiene. Red Deer, Alberta, is home for Lori, her husband, Brent, and their two adult children, Michael and Olivia. Lori's hobbies include working out with a personal trainer, hiking in the Rocky Mountains with her husband, and going on coffee dates with friends.

www.ingramcontent.com/pod-product-compliance
Lightning Source LLC
Chambersburg PA
CBHW030818210726
48290CB00002B/643